The Little Mexican Donkey Boy

THE LITTLE MEXICAN DONKEY BOY

The LITTLE MEXICAN DONKEY BOY

BY
MADELINE BRANDEIS

❧

Photographic Illustrations

❧

GROSSET & DUNLAP
PUBLISHERS   NEW YORK
by arrangement with the A. Flanagan Company

PRINTED IN THE UNITED STATES OF AMERICA

PREFACE

When I began to write these stories about children of all lands I had just returned from Europe whither I journeyed with Marie and Ref. Maybe you don't·know Marie and Ref. I'll introduce them: Please meet Marie, my very little daughter, and Ref, my very big reflex camera.

These two are my helpers. Marie helps by being a little girl who knows what other little girls like and by telling me; and Ref helps by snapping pictures of everything interesting that Marie and I see on our travels. I couldn't get along without them.

Several years have gone by since we started our work together and Marie is a bigger girl—but Ref hasn't changed one bit. Ref hasn't changed any more than my interest in writing these books for you. And I hope that *you* hope that I'll never change, because I want to keep on writing until we'll have no more countries to write about—unless, of course, some one discovers a new country.

Even if a new country isn't discovered, we'll find foreign children to talk about—maybe the children

in Mars! Who knows? Nobody. Not even Marie—
and Marie usually knows about most things. That's
the reason why, you see, though I sign myself

Madeline Brandeis

I am really only

Marie's Mother.

"THANK YOU" NOTE

If it had not been for some of my friends I could not have illustrated THE LITTLE MEXICAN DONKEY BOY.

To you, my dear Mrs. de Lecuona, go my most fervent thanks for the kind help you have given me and for the photographs which you have allowed me to reproduce in this book.

John Tapia, who posed as Dodo—thank you for being so like my little hero and for letting me photograph you. It is needless to tell the reader that you are a real Mexican boy.

Lois Jane Campbell and Helen Claire McAllister—you have brought Dolores and Felicia to life very charmingly and I am grateful to you.

José Herrera of the "Durango" booth in the Mexican street of Los Angeles—that delightful El Paseo—you have made a striking Señor and I appreciate your help.

John Brandreth—I know you didn't want to fight with a girl but you did do it splendidly nevertheless, proving that you are a good actor and a very accommodating friend. Thank you, John.

For the real Mexican pottery used in some of the scenes and for the guitar, I am indebted to my good friend, Adolph Fleischman, and to my good mother, Mrs. Albert Frank.

Madeline Brandeis

CONTENTS

MEXICAN BOYS DRESSED IN CHARRO COSTUMES

The Little Mexican Donkey Boy

CHAPTER I

DODO

"Wake up, lazy one! Today something very splendid is going to happen!"

A clear voice rang out on the early morning air.

A stout brown woman leaned over a sleeping brown boy. She prodded him with a little switch and scolded.

"Up, up, I say! You have slept long enough!"

The boy turned over lazily and looked around. He could see that the morning was very young. He could see that it was earlier than his usual rising time.

He slept upon the floor. He was wrapped

11

DODO

up in a bright-colored blanket. He rubbed his eyes.

"Yah, ha," he yawned, "I'm coming. I'm coming."

But his motions were slow. The great woman above him walked away.

As she walked she called back, "Then

hurry. Your breakfast is waiting and there is much to do today."

The boy yawned and stretched as he made ready for breakfast. He was a good-looking lad with black eyes and hair. His face was brown, for he was a Mexican. Many Mexicans are brown. That is because they are part Indian and part Spanish.

Some of the people in Mexico are Indians and are called peons. They are the laborers of Mexico. The stout woman was a peon.

Some of the rich and powerful people are full-blooded Spaniards.

But this boy was a mestizo (mĕs-tē′zō). The mestizos are part Spanish and part Indian. They call themselves the "new race." The people of this new race hope to build up Mexico. They hope to do for their country what the Americans did for the United States.

But of course, this boy was not thinking of that. In fact, Dodo did not think very

HE SLEPT ON THE FLOOR

much of anything. Yes, he thought of breakfast and dinner and any other meal he could eat. But after that, he was not interested in anything.

"Have you washed your face and put on your sandals?" called the woman.

Dodo hurried just a little.

"I'm coming," he said.

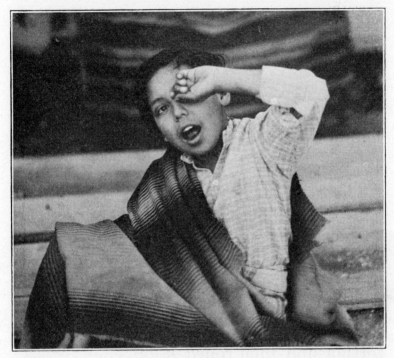

HE YAWNED

In the kitchen he squatted on the bare floor. The stout woman knelt by a charcoal stove and made tortillas (tōr-tēl′yäs). These are flat pancakes of corn.

Clap, clap! The woman clapped some dough from the palm of one hand to the other. Then she baked the round dough on a flat earthenware plate over the fire. The tortillas are the bread of the Mexicans.

Dodo was the last one to enter the room. The others were already eating. There were five other persons there besides Dodo.

One was a dark, wrinkled man with a long, black mustache. He was the husband of the stout woman.

The others were small brown children. They all ate quietly. They did not speak. They looked at Dodo with their black eyes. The oldest boy rolled his tortilla and ate it that way. The father put some beans in his tortilla and then rolled it up.

Suddenly the mother broke the silence.

She said, "Tell him, Manuel (măn'ū-ĕl), what you are doing today."

Manuel, the father, swallowed a mouthful and began to talk in a low, deep voice.

"We go on a little journey today, Dodo, you and I," he said.

AN INDIAN FAMILY

For just a moment Dodo's dreamy, dark eyes brightened. But then they drooped again. He simply answered, "Si (sē)," which means yes in Spanish. Then he went on with his breakfast.

Now the strange part was that any other boy in Dodo's place would have whooped with joy at this news. For Dodo had not left the ranch where he lived in many and many a long month; and a Mexican ranch is a very lonely, quiet place.

In Mexico a ranch is called a hacienda (hä-sĭ-ĕn′dä). This hacienda belonged to a Spanish gentleman who lived in the United States. He lived in the state of California. Occasionally the gentleman visited his large hacienda. But most of the time it was Manuel who managed it for him.

The gentleman trusted Manuel. Manuel worked very hard on the hacienda. Manuel and his family lived in a tiny house. But the large, empty house of the Spanish gentleman stood on a hill in the center of the ranch.

"Are you not happy to take this trip, Dodo?" asked Manuel's wife.

She could not understand why the boy was not more interested. He was never interested and always sleepy. He had been called Dodo because of that. For Dodo is a nickname in Spanish for "little sleepy-

DODO LIKED TO EAT TORTILLAS

head." Nobody ever remembered Dodo's real name, not even Dodo himself.

"I shall be glad," he answered. But he did not seem glad the way an American child would.

Manuel, the father, explained, "We go to the village to buy provisions for the big house. Yesterday I received a letter from

the Señor Gallego (sā-nyōr′ Gäl-yā′gō). Soon
he is coming. Everything must be made
ready.''

When Manuel spoke of Señor Gallego, he
meant the gentleman who owned the
hacienda. "Señor" is gentleman in Spanish.

So the great Señor of the hacienda was
coming! Dodo liked to think about the
Señor. He liked to think lazily about the
Señor's life in the big house on the hill. That
must be a very pleasant life.

Dodo disliked the idea of growing older
and having to work hard in the fields. Often
Manuel would come home very tired and
hot. Often he would not come home to his
tiny shack until his family were all asleep.

Manuel had to work very hard. But the
Señor from the United States always dressed
in cool white clothes and did not work.
Dodo liked that. Dodo wanted to grow up
and not have to work. But he knew that it
could not be.

HE WAS A VERY LAZY BOY

Yet, Dodo was not the real son of Manuel, the peon, and his stout wife. He did not really belong there in that little house with those other brown children.

But he had lived there ever since he could remember. He did not know who his parents were. He only knew that he was a mestizo, while Manuel and his family were pure Indians.

This, however, made no difference to Dodo. He loved Manuel and the stout Indian woman as much as he could love anyone. For he was a very lazy, sleepy boy. He was not interested in anything.

CHAPTER II

THE SERVANT

On the trip, Manuel was very quiet. Dodo never spoke very much at any time. They drove an old wagon. But the horses were splendid. Dodo enjoyed watching their graceful movements. While watching, his eyes grew heavy and he nodded.

Manuel smiled. "Come," he said, "try to keep awake until we reach the town. You will be interested in what we shall see there."

Dodo opened one eye. Then he closed it again. He would have been in the land of Nod had not Manuel continued, "You do not yet know all about the Señor's visit."

At the word "Señor," the boy sat up a little straighter and listened.

23

"The Señor does not come alone this time," explained Manuel. "This time he brings his family to the hacienda."

"Si?" asked Dodo. He was but slightly interested. Women and children did not mean very much to him.

"Si," replied Manuel. "He brings his two daughters, the Señoritas (sā′nyō-rē′täs) Dolores (dō-lō′rēz) and Felicia (fē-lĭsh′ĭ-å). And also the Señora (sā-nyō′rä) Gallego, his wife."

This news only made Dodo sleepier. He was about to doze off again when he heard words that made him start with displeasure. Manuel was talking, and this time Manuel's voice was stern.

"It is time you learned to be of use, sleepy one," the man said. "The two Señoritas will need a servant, a mozo (mō′zō). You shall be that mozo!"

Dodo jumped. "Eh? I? A mozo?" he squealed with fright.

NO MORE COULD HE DREAM

"Si," answered Manuel. "What is so terrible about that?"

Dodo could not answer. His heart had sunk down, down, almost, he thought, to his toes.

So two young girls were coming to the hacienda! The Señor Gallego was bringing his two young daughters! And he, Dodo, was to wait upon them! While the Señor walked about in white clothes, Dodo was to wait upon the two young daughters!

No more could Dodo lounge in the shade of the alligator-pear tree. No more could he curl up beside the door with his legs drawn up to his chin, and dream until he fell asleep.

He saw himself running back and forth. He felt himself hot and tired. He heard shrill voices calling, "Hi, Dodo, my fan!" Or, "Mozo, bring the chocolate to the roof!" Or, "Fetch my pony!"

Oh, they would drive him until he should fall in his tracks! Poor lazy, sleepy Dodo!

"Do not look as if the end of the world had come, foolish boy," laughed Manuel. "This will be the making of you. At last, here is a job to limber up your lazy bones!"

As Manuel laughed he showed all his white, glistening teeth under the black mustache.

Dodo could not sleep now. The joy had all

gone out of his life. He must soon work. He sulked and did not see the beautiful country through which they were passing.

He did not see the fine fields of corn, the bright flower gardens, the tall prickly cactus, and the great palm trees. For Mexico is a land of sunshine and beauty.

Great mountains are in Mexico—the Sierra Madre (sĭ-ĕr′ȧ mä′drā) Mountains, meaning "mother range."

But Dodo's thoughts were not of mountains and flowers and trees. He was very angry inside of him.

Often Dodo had heard about the bullfights in Mexico City and he had wanted to see one. All boys thought the bullfights fine things. The bullfighters were brave, and dressed in handsome uniforms, and everyone admired them. Sometimes they rode on horses.

Dodo began to think, "I would rather be a bullfighter than anything else in the world.

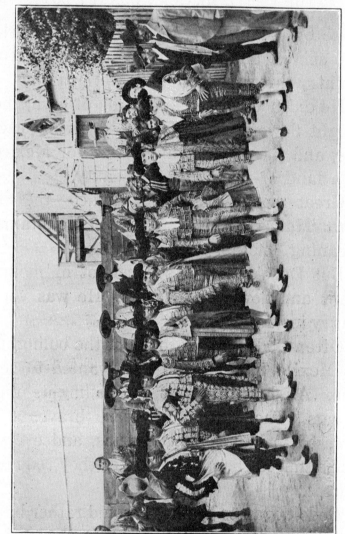

THE BULLFIGHTERS WERE BRAVE

Of course, I would rather be nothing at all. But if I must work, then I shall be a bull-fighter!"

He began to wonder how he could escape Manuel and go to Mexico City. He did not stop to think that children cannot become bullfighters. He did not know, either, what a terrible thing a bullfight is.

He only thought one thought, "I shall not be a mozo for the Señor's daughters!"

"We shall buy some new white trousers for you, Dodo," said Manuel. "You must look your best for the Señor's young ladies!"

Dodo glanced at his old patched cotton trousers. He had only this pair and another even more patched and old. Once a week his foster-mother took them to the stream and washed them. They were quite comfortable and Dodo did not want a new pair. He was fond of his old clothes.

He took off his big, turned-up straw hat

and looked at it. It was torn in places and faded. But Dodo loved it.

He was thinking, "They will not allow me to wear this. I shall have to wear a new, stiff sombrero (sŏm-brā′rō)."

A sombrero is what the Mexican calls his large hat. Most Mexicans prize their hats and like to buy the finest they can afford. Sometimes they save their money for many years in order to buy a sombrero.

But Dodo did not like new things. He was content with the old. He was content, too, with his life. He did not want to be a mozo.

"The sombrero is not very pretty, eh?" spoke Manuel, looking at Dodo's faded hat. "But we cannot afford a new one."

"It does not matter," snapped Dodo.

"Ay, what ails you, boy?" Manuel inquired. "Are you not proud that you are to serve such highborn Señoritas? Many a fellow would envy you!"

But this only made Dodo angrier. "I shall

THE MEXICAN INDIANS LOVE CHILDREN

not work," he thought, "and I am not a peon. I do not have to serve the Spaniard."

Dodo was thinking and feeling as many other Mexicans have thought and felt. But he did not know how foolish he was to feel that way.

A more sensible boy would have reasoned, "But what else can I do? I should be glad that some one has cared for me and is helping me."

For Dodo knew quite well the story of his life. As a tiny baby he had been left at the Cuna (kōo′nä), a Mexican orphan asylum. The word "cuna" means cradle in Spanish. The good Sisters at this Cuna always try to find homes for the babies left them.

Often they give these orphans to Indian women and pay the Indian women to care for them. They do this because they know how much an Indian loves children.

This is what had happened in the case of Dodo. He had been left at the Cuna. The

Sisters had given him to the care of Manuel's wife.

At that time there had been no little Manuels, and Dodo was welcomed at the hacienda. But even after Manuel's own babies came, Dodo was treated just the same as before.

Dodo should have been a very grateful boy. He should have wanted to help Manuel, his kind foster-father. He should have been pleased to stay on the hacienda and serve the Señoritas who were coming, instead of wanting to run away and become a bull-fighter.

CHAPTER III

THE LITTLE ONE

They came to the town. Like most Mexican towns, it was built around a plaza, or public square. On Sundays and Thursdays this square became a market place. Indians from the country came to town with their wares. They sat under umbrellas right out in the street and waited for people to buy. They waited very patiently.

These plazas started in the olden days when people from different villages would meet to trade and talk. To the plaza would come cloth weavers from one village, farmers from another, and potters from another. So the plaza came to be born. Today it is an important part of Mexican city life.

The town to which Manuel and Dodo came

34

A MEXICAN PLAZA

was a village of potters. Almost every man in that village made pottery. Almost every man's father had made pottery. And almost every man's grandfather and great-grandfather had made it, too.

So that was why, as Dodo and Manuel made their way through the narrow streets, they saw even little children modeling clay. These little children would grow up to be potters some day. And so would their children.

It was all very quiet and sleepy in the town. There is a saying, "In Mexico nothing ever changes." This may be true. But still, some things have changed. For Mexico has had terrible battles and much disorder and unhappiness. The people have revolted. Yet they seem so quiet and gentle. But in their eyes there is a black fire.

Manuel went to the market place and bought many things. Dodo watched him sleepily. He envied the lazy Indians who

A MEXICAN FRUIT MARKET

squatted beside their little piles of oranges and mangoes and other fruits and flowers and wares. That seemed an easy life.

The ice cream man passed.

"Nieve! Nieve (nē-ā′vä)!" he called.

That meant snow. They call ice cream snow in Mexico. The ice cream man carried a bucket on his head. Dodo wanted some ice cream. But he was too lazy to ask for it.

They went to see a potter. Manuel must buy some pretty Mexican pottery for the Señor's daughters. The Señor had asked for it in his letter.

There were water bottles and jars, pitchers and dishes. They were newly made and the potter had arranged them in a row. A woman was sitting upon the ground painting a large jar. She painted with a brush made of hairs from a dog's tail. The colors were bright and attractive.

Dodo suddenly became interested. He drew closer to the woman. He watched si-

A MEXICAN VARIETY SHOP

lently while Manuel traded with the potter. Dodo admired the graceful shapes of those bright-colored jars. He was fascinated. Never before had he longed to do anything as he now longed to touch those beautiful things. He wanted to snatch the brush out of the woman's hand and paint that jar himself. But he only stood silently and watched.

Finally the woman put down the jar. She reached for another. While she was reaching, Dodo's hand shot out and he started to grab the jar. He did not understand why he did this thing. But he did it. Before he could think, the woman's hand came down on his with a loud slap.

Dodo drew back in alarm. But the woman's face was not angry.

She said, "That was not for you, that slap. It was for your meddling hands. Hands should not meddle." Then she smiled a smile that told Dodo how much she loved little children.

Courtesy of Southern Pacific Co.

A QUAINT SIDEWALK BAZAAR

Dodo moved closer again. Then the woman, still smiling, gave him a tiny clay dish with a chicken painted on it.

"Take this," she said, "and play with it."

Dodo did not want to play. He was too old to play with a clay dish that had a chicken painted on it. But somehow, he had always been too old for that.

Mexican children seem to be born old. They seldom shout or make a noise. Even the babies hardly ever cry. They do not know how to play the way we do.

But Dodo took the dish. He took it with him and he went into the shade and stood beside the wall looking at it. He leaned against the wall in his favorite position with his feet crossed.

One might have thought that Dodo feared lest the houses tumble down. He seemed to want to lean against them all to hold them up. But that was only his laziness.

Now he studied the dish. It was thin and

HE LEANED AGAINST THE WALL

beautifully made. Dodo knew that he, too, could make a dish like that. He felt it. He also felt that he could paint prettier designs than the Indian woman painted.

He strolled back.

"Will you let me paint?" he asked the woman suddenly.

Manuel was still buying from the potter. Dodo could see his broad back inside the little house. He could hear the two men arguing.

"Si, niño (nēn'yō)," answered the Indian woman pleasantly. What she meant was, "Yes, little one." She handed Dodo a newly made jar, a very small one.

She watched the boy as he took up a brush and began to paint. She was ready to laugh at his clumsiness. But he surprised her when he did not smear the colors or drop the brush.

He worked carefully and painted a design. It was, of course, a very simple design. But it was as neatly done as any of the woman's designs. She was indeed surprised.

"You will yet be an artist, niño," she laughed. Then she turned to her work and forgot Dodo.

But Dodo did not forget the pottery. He sat and longed to do more.

"Come, we will go now," called Manuel.
But Dodo did not move.

"He likes to watch the painting, eh?" laughed the potter. "Let him stay while you finish your shopping in the town. Then you may call for him again."

That was how Dodo happened to stay at the potter's house. While Manuel was gone, the boy watched and longed more every minute to do the interesting work of a potter.

Then he thought of a plan. He might become a potter. In this way he would not have to go back to the hacienda and wait upon the Señoritas.

"I should like to stay here with you and learn your trade," said Dodo to the potter.

The potter did not laugh now. He looked grave and shook his head.

"No," he answered. "We do not need more potters, niño. We have many children of our own and two grown sons who now work quite well. Go home and follow the trade of your father."

DODO'S MASTER WAS ART

"But I have no father," said Dodo quietly.

"No father?" exclaimed the potter. "But Manuel? Is Manuel not your father?"

Dodo told him his story. The potter looked at Dodo a long time without talking.

Then he stroked the boy's black hair and said, "Nevertheless, niño, you must go back to the hacienda and serve your master."

Dodo's heart throbbed at these words.

He thought, "I have no master!"

But he did have a master; though, of course, he did not know it. The potter did not know it. Neither did Manuel. For Dodo's master was Art.

CHAPTER IV

THE LITTLE JAR

Manuel came back for Dodo later on. But the potter said that the boy had disappeared.

"Soon after you left," said the potter, "he was not here. We thought he went to join you."

Manuel scratched his head.

"I have not seen him in the town," he puzzled.

They searched the potter's house. They looked in the garden.

The potter's daughter told them, "The niño passed me with a little jar in his hands."

But she did not know where the niño had gone.

Photo by Keystone View Co.

AN OVEN FOR POTTERY—IN BACKGROUND ARE BRANCHES OF ORGAN
CACTUS USED AS FUEL IN THE OVEN

Then Manuel again scratched his head.

"I hope he is not stealing," said poor Manuel.

"Do not worry," the potter comforted Manuel. "The niño will come back. He is only charmed by this new art. He has never before seen so interesting a work and it has taken his fancy. He will soon tire of his new toy."

But the potter and Manuel did not know that this was not a toy to Dodo. This was very serious indeed. To Dodo, little sleepy Dodo, here, at last, was something interesting. Here, at last, was something very interesting and beautiful.

Of course Dodo did not know why this was. He did not know that many years ago his own father had been a potter and had lived in this very town. Nobody knew that. But it was true. Art had been the master of Dodo's father. And Art was Dodo's master, too.

So Manuel stayed at the potter's house and waited. But no Dodo came back.

By a stream under a palm tree sat the little boy, Dodo. In his fingers was a dog's hair brush. With his brown fingers he was using that brush to paint a picture on an earthen jar. He did not know that the day was going by. He did not know that Manuel was waiting to take him home.

Manuel had bought new white trousers and a belt for Dodo. He even had a bag of candy tucked away in his pocket.

"I must go back to the hacienda," said Manuel at last. "It grows late, and there is much for me to do there. You must send the boy home by someone who goes that way."

"Si," answered the potter. "I shall send him to you. He will surely come back."

But Manuel felt very strange about going home without Dodo. Still, what could he do?

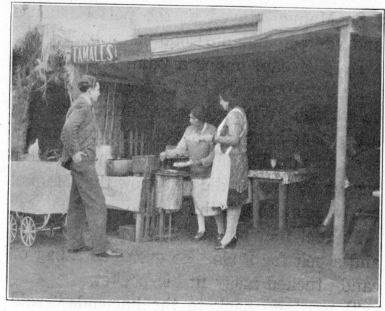

A COOKING BOOTH

So the good man went to the market place once more. He looked about to be sure that Dodo was not there. Then he bought himself a tamale (tá-mä'lĕ) which is a very peppery combination of meat and crushed corn wrapped up in corn husks.

He bought this tamale from a woman who was cooking right there in the market place.

She had a little charcoal stove, and the odor of food came from her booth.

Manuel finished his meal. Then he wrapped his blanket around him. He wore the regular Mexican blanket. It hung folded over his shoulder all day. But when the weather turned cold he wrapped it about him.

Manuel started home without Dodo.

Now, when it grew darker, Dodo looked up from his painting. He felt all stiff and cramped. He had been sitting in the same position for so long.

But a wide smile slowly spread over his bronze face. His white teeth shone. And his sleepy, drooping eyes were not sleepy and drooping at all. They now sparkled.

He had made a beautiful picture on the water jar. It pleased him so that he had to smile with joy.

He went back to the potter's house. He had completely forgotten Manuel. He was a little surprised to find the sky so dark. He was also surprised to see the potter and his family seated about the stove eating their dinner. They sat under the trees. They ate silently like Manuel's family.

"Where is Manuel?" asked Dodo of the potter.

"He has gone home," answered the potter.

Dodo was startled and a trifle afraid. But then he looked again at the lovely little painted jar in his hands. The fear left him.

"See," he said, as he held out the jar to the potter, "I have painted a picture upon the little jar."

The potter stretched out his hand and took the jar. He looked at it carefully. Then he looked at Dodo in a strange way. His black eyes were half closed.

He said, "So this is what you have been doing. And did you not know that the Señor Manuel was waiting for you?"

Dodo did not know. How could he have

known? He had forgotten everything but that little jar.

"No, I did not think that the time passed so quickly," replied the boy.

The potter turned the jar over in his hands and examined it. But he did not speak. Dodo could stand it no longer.

"Do you not think it beautiful, Señor?" he asked, while his whole face lit up with pleasure.

It was growing darker all the time. The potter's wife and the potter's children tried to see Dodo's design upon the jar. But they could not see it.

The potter held it close to the fire. Still he said nothing. Dodo thought his breath would stop coming. He waited, and it seemed years. Then at last the potter spoke. He spoke slowly and he told a great lie.

He said, "It is not good at all. It is poorly made."

Now, the potter had a reason for saying

A MEXICAN FLOWER MARKET

what he did. The potter had two sons who were learning his trade. And two very stupid boys they were.

This work of Dodo's was unusually good. It showed that Dodo had a real love for the art. The potter's sons had love only for pleasure.

Dodo had made a beautiful design without practice, while the potter's own sons had practiced for years and could not do a work like this. The potter knew it and became very jealous of Dodo.

"Manuel has told me to send you home," said the potter to Dodo. "You must leave tomorrow morning with the first man who goes that way."

But Dodo's eyes began to snap.

"No," he cried, "I will not go."

The potter smiled.

"Sit down and eat," he invited the boy, not unkindly. "Come, Marie, give the niño some beans and a tortilla."

But Dodo could not eat. He had a great lump in his throat.

"I will not go back to the hacienda," he said. His voice was choking with tears. "I will stay here and learn to be a potter!"

CHAPTER V

"I AM GOING"

In the morning the potter's wife examined Dodo's jar.

"It is beautiful," she said to the potter. "I believe it is as good as any of yours."

This speech made the jealous potter more jealous than ever.

"The boy goes back to Manuel today," he said shortly.

But the wife felt sorry for Dodo.

"Let him stay," she pleaded. "He is a good lad and will help with the work."

"No," the potter growled, "his painting will surely be admired. With practice his work will be better than that of Pedro (pā′drō) and Juan (hwän)." Those were the names of the potter's sons.

59

But still the wife insisted. "Tell the boy
he must work for us, and then you will
teach him to paint. Tell him he must become your mozo, and you will pay him by
teaching."

The potter seemed pleased with this idea.
He was a poor man and he had never had
his own mozo.

"That is not such a bad plan," he agreed.

So to Dodo he said, "You may stay here
and learn my trade. But you must be my
mozo and serve me."

The word "mozo" did not please Dodo at
all. But he was so anxious to paint and learn
to model in clay that he answered willingly,
"Si, si, I shall do as you say. Only let me
learn the art."

The potter smiled and nodded his head.
Then he walked off and began to think.
The potter was not a kind man like Manuel.
He did not want Dodo to become a potter.
He was afraid that Dodo might become a

MEXICAN GIRLS ON A HACIENDA

better potter than his own sons. And he was very jealous.

So he said to himself, "The boy shall work very hard for me. He shall be sent to the market place. He shall do all the work of Pedro and Juan. Then Pedro and Juan may use their time for learning my trade."

But poor little Dodo did not know what a plan this potter was scheming. Dodo thought only of being a potter and of living here in this village of potters.

So he sent word to Manuel that he was not coming home.

He sent word that he was staying to become the potter's mozo.

Manuel said to his wife, "He is a strange boy. He refused to serve the high-born Señoritas. But he willingly becomes the mozo of a common potter."

Manuel's wife shrugged her shoulders and replied, "Ah, wait and see. He will not stay. He will not be the mozo to anyone.

He is far too lazy, too sleepy. Ah, little sleepyhead!"

She waddled into the house chuckling to herself. She knew her Dodo.

But for many days the boy worked hard for the potter. He went to market carrying great loads of the potter's water jars. He sold them in the market square.

He did all the work of Pedro and Juan. He was kept busy all day long.

But he did not mind because he knew he was earning his lessons.

Sometimes the potter did teach him. But often he disappointed the boy.

He would say, "No, not tonight, niño. No lesson tonight. I am too tired. Tomorrow."

Then Dodo would go to bed very sad, and very tired, and very discouraged.

Sometimes Dodo would go to the mountain charcoal pits for charcoal to burn in the stove. He might make many trips a day. He would pile the charcoal on top of the little patient donkey and bring it home to the potter's wife.

Gradually Dodo began to tire of so much work. He still loved to paint and model in clay, but he began to wonder if it were worth all this work.

Then, too, the potter discouraged him. The potter sometimes laughed at Dodo's designs when really they were well done. The potter knew it. But he was very jealous.

One day a wealthy traveler came to the village. The potter sold him a handsome set of dishes.

He told the traveler that he, the potter, had painted those dishes himself. This was not true.

Dodo had painted those dishes and had worked over them for many a day.

He had painted the Mexican emblem on all of them. The Mexican emblem is an eagle perched upon a cactus eating a serpent.

There is a story about this strange emblem.

An old Aztec Indian god told his people to wander over the land until they found an eagle perched upon a cactus eating a serpent.

If they found such a bird they might know that here was the spot upon which to build their great city.

It was near the shore of Lake Texcoco (tās-kō′kō) that they saw the eagle. He sat upon a cactus and had in his beak a writhing snake. So the people settled there and began to build the city of Mexico.

Of course Dodo knew this story and he liked the emblem. He painted it upon the dishes.

When the traveler came, Dodo heard the potter say, "That is one of my best designs. I spent many weeks working on this set of dishes."

Dodo's face grew red with anger and hurt

INDIAN WOMEN CARRYING WATER

pride. He felt the potter's unfairness. He also knew that the man was doing a great wrong.

When the traveler left, Dodo stood before the potter with his dark eyes gleaming.

"You have told a falsehood," he said quietly.

The potter stopped counting the money he had received from the traveler. He looked at Dodo and scowled.

"Go about your work, rude one," he commanded, "and leave me to mine."

"That was not your work, that which you have just sold," said Dodo. "It was mine."

The potter did not answer at all. He finished counting his money and then sat down upon the stump of a tree. He beckoned Dodo to his side.

"Come here," he said.

Dodo moved closer to the potter. But he was still very angry and his face was still very red.

"Do you wish to stay here and learn to be a potter?" asked the man.

"You know that I do," answered Dodo.

"Then you must do as I say," the potter continued. "You must agree to make what I tell you to make. When I sell your work you must say nothing."

"And you will tell people that they are your works?" asked the boy.

"Si, I shall," the man replied firmly.

Dodo was stunned. He really did not mind so much having the potter sell the things without telling who made them. It was not that.

But Dodo despised falsehoods. He despised hearing the potter telling people falsehoods.

Still he wanted to stay. So he had to agree to this unfair plan.

The days went by. It made Dodo very unhappy to watch his own carefully made works selling as the works of the potter.

WASH DAY IN A MEXICAN VILLAGE

Then one day something happened and Dodo could stand it no longer.

A lady came to town and admired a graceful jug which Dodo had painted. Juan, one of the potter's sons, was standing near-by.

Dodo heard the potter say to the lady, "Si, that is the finest jug we have. The design was painted by my youngest son, Juan."

Juan giggled foolishly. But he did not seem to mind the terrible untruth that his father had told.

The lady was pleased to hear that such a young boy had done this lovely work. So she bought the jug and paid a high price for it.

Dodo then went into the house and folded up his little blanket, his serape (sĕ-rä′pā). He also folded his other pair of trousers and his cotton shirt.

After that he went into the garden and

HE THANKED HER AND LEFT

found the potter's wife preparing lunch by the side of the little stove.

"I am going," said the boy.

The potter's wife looked up. She was fond of Dodo. She knew he was a good boy. She also knew that her husband had been unfair to him.

"Why?" she asked kindly. "Are you not happy?"

Dodo answered, "No, I am not happy. And I am going."

The potter's wife only said, "I am sorry." That was all. She did not try to keep Dodo. She did not even kiss him goodbye.

She naturally thought he was going home. She gave him a few coins and a lump of clay to take along. He thanked her and left.

But Dodo was not going home. He had tried being a mozo and he did not like it.

He was now in a terrible position. He could not stay at the potter's and learn the trade he loved so well because he was being treated unfairly.

And he would not go back to the hacienda because there they would make him work as a mozo.

Dodo was between the frying pan and the fire.

CHAPTER VI

THE LITTLE DONKEY

Dodo did not go home. Once more he determined to make his way to Mexico City and become a bullfighter. Why learn to be a potter when one must work as a mozo? Why work as a mozo when one must listen to lies?

No, he would go to Mexico City, and there he would find out about the famous bullfights.

The bullfight is a sport greatly enjoyed by a large number of Mexican people. Dodo had never seen one but he felt sure that he should like it.

So he started his journey. He started to walk along the hot road. Soon he stopped at a tiny hut where Indians lived. They

74

gave him tortillas. He thanked them and went on his way.

It was very warm and he walked lazily. He did not like to walk. But he must. There was no other way.

All at once he saw before him a strange sight. There, in the middle of the road, he saw a boy and a donkey. The boy was about his own age. He was a peon, a peasant.

The donkey was small and gray. On his back was a heavy load.

The peon boy was screaming and hitting the little donkey. But the donkey refused to move.

"Get on! Hi! Move, beast of evil. Move!" screamed the angry boy. His face was hot and red. His voice was husky from screaming.

Dodo approached. He knew just how that donkey felt. He felt that way himself. He felt as though he could not walk another step. And he was not forced to carry a

THE DONKEY

heavy load such as the poor donkey carried.

Dodo sat down on the side of the road and watched the scene before him. He took off his large straw hat and mopped his brow.

Suddenly the peon boy noticed Dodo.

"Why do you not help me?" he asked with tears in his voice. "I cannot make him move."

"That I see," answered Dodo, smiling. But he did not offer to help.

"Come and help me," demanded the boy.

Dodo shook his head.

"It is no use trying," he replied. "The donkey will not move, and I cannot blame him for that."

The peon boy came over and threw himself down beside Dodo. He was worn out and panting.

"He is a stubborn, lazy donkey," complained the boy, almost crying. "He has acted this way before. If I do not take my father's pottery to market I shall be beaten!"

Dodo noticed that the load upon the donkey's back consisted of red water jars. This boy's father was, no doubt, a potter. He had sent the boy to town to sell his wares.

But Dodo knew that the boy would never reach that town—not if the donkey had anything to say about it.

"If only I could find some one to buy the lazy creature! I would sell him for so little. He is useless, useless!" the boy raged.

"Your father would not allow you to sell the donkey," said Dodo.

"Yes, yes," the peon cried. "He has said so! But who would want a lazy thing like that? Who?"

Dodo pondered. "Maybe a lazy person would," he reflected.

Then he asked the boy, "How much do you want for him?"

"Oh, anything," replied the other, carelessly. Then he looked at Dodo quickly. "But why do you ask?" he added.

Dodo shrugged his shoulders. "Oh, because I might like to buy him myself," he said.

"You?" inquired the boy, surprised. He

ONE WAY OF TRAVELING IN MEXICO

looked at Dodo's patched trousers and faded shirt.

"Si," Dodo answered thoughtfully. "That is, if you do not ask too much."

The boy grew interested. Then he mentioned a sum of money which he said his father would take for the donkey. It was very little for a donkey. But to Dodo it was a great deal.

"Still, I will buy him," Dodo announced. He felt in his pocket for the few coins which the potter's wife had given him.

"I can pay you only a few coins now," he said. "But I shall send you the rest from Mexico City."

"From Mexico City?" exclaimed the peon, puzzled.

"Yes, I go there to be a bullfighter," Dodo told him calmly. "I shall soon have plenty of money. Then I shall send you what I owe for the donkey."

"Oh!" breathed the peon with surprise.

He did not doubt Dodo's word. He was just a country boy. He knew no more about bullfights than Dodo did. He believed the strange lad with the drooping eyes.

But the peon could hardly believe that he was really talking with a bullfighter. He did not stop to think that Dodo had only said he was "going to be a bullfighter."

The peon could already see his companion in the bull-ring dressed in a velvet suit with gold braid. Dodo was rather tall for his age and he stood very straight. In spite of his lazy ways, he was a fine, upright-looking lad.

"That is settled then," said Dodo. "Now we must unload the donkey."

"But my father's wares? How shall I get them to town?" demanded the peon.

Dodo replied, "We shall take the baskets from the donkey's back. I shall carry one and you the other."

The boy's mouth dropped open.

HE COULD RIDE COMFORTABLY ON THE DONKEY'S BACK

"What?" he cried, "We carry the baskets of pottery while the donkey's back goes free?"

"It is the only way to do," said Dodo.

He started to unfasten the huge baskets. One hung on either side of the little animal. Both were piled with much heavy pottery.

The donkey stood quietly. His eyes were closed. But when he felt the load slip from his back he opened one eye and looked around. Dodo showed his glistening teeth in a broad smile.

"That is better, si?" he laughed as he stroked the donkey's soft gray neck.

"At last," thought the donkey (if donkeys think), "at last I have found a boy who understands!"

"Now, come," said Dodo to the peon, "you lift one and I the other."

It was a strange thing for a boy nicknamed "Sleepyhead" to do. But Dodo wanted that donkey. He saw a way of traveling which would be more pleasant on hot days. He could ride comfortably on the donkey's back.

Perhaps, too, Dodo felt a very natural sympathy for the tired little donkey. Perhaps Dodo and the donkey were much alike. One thing was certain. They were to become staunch friends.

CHAPTER VII

HAPPINESS AND SORROW

Let us leave Dodo and his new friend, the donkey. Let us go now to our own country, the United States. Let us visit the Señor Gallego who owned the hacienda where Dodo had lived all his life.

The Gallego family lived in California, Mexico's neighbor. They lived in Los Angeles which is a Spanish name and means "The Angels." That is the reason this city is sometimes called the "City of Angels."

California is full of Spanish names and Spanish people. That is because California was first settled by the Spaniards. Yet, even in California, the American children do not know very much about their southern neighbors, the Mexicans.

85

Señor Gallego had two little girls. They were those same Señoritas whom Manuel was expecting at the hacienda. They were the young ladies that Dodo had been expected to serve. They were really the cause of Dodo's flight. But of course these two little girls were unaware of all this. They had never even heard of Dodo.

The last day of school had arrived. The Gallego sisters were dressing. They were very much excited. It was small wonder, for today they were going to the school celebration; and tomorrow they were leaving for Mexico.

"Hurry, Dolores," cried her sister, Felicia. "See! I am all ready."

Felicia stood before the mirror in the girls' dainty room. She looked at herself in the mirror very proudly. She had reason to be proud for she was a beautiful little girl.

She had lovely golden curls and her eyes were brown. She was a real Spanish girl,

DOLORES AND FELICIA

even though she did not look like the Spanish girls we imagine. But it is true that in
Spain there are many people with blond
hair.

"I am ready, Felicia," answered her sister,
Dolores.

Dolores was not like Felicia, though the
two were twins. Dolores' eyes were dark
and bright and her hair was coal black. She

looked like pictures we see of true Spanish Señoritas. Dolores had a sweeter expression, even though her face was not so pretty as her sister's.

The two little girls were dressed in Spanish costumes. Their costumes had belonged to their grandmother who had lived in Spain.

Their mother and father had lived in Mexico before the twins were born. But there had been terrible fighting and revolutions in Mexico.

So Señor Gallego had moved his delicate wife away. He had brought her to Los Angeles where Dolores and Felicia had been born.

"Our costumes will be the best," said Felicia, as they drove to school in their father's big automobile.

"Maybe not," answered Dolores. "You know there are other children whose parents came from Spain and Mexico. They may have pretty costumes, too."

"Not so rich and grand as ours!" Felicia replied.

She held her head high. She wore a beautiful white mantilla, which is a lace scarf, held in place by a tall comb. Felicia's light hair looked like spun gold under the lace.

Dolores wore a black mantilla. Her black hair shone beneath it.

The school held a fiesta (fyĕs'tä), or Spanish festival, each year. It was the regular closing day celebration. They had Spanish food, and Spanish music, and Spanish plays.

A prize was always given for the best costume.

Felicia had won the prize the year before. She was quite certain that she would win it again this year.

But Felicia was a great worry to her sister, Dolores.

The little dark girl sometimes wondered how such a beautiful child as Felicia could be so unpleasant.

THE SCHOOL HELD A FIESTA

For Felicia was selfish. She was not only selfish, but she was proud and willful. She often made people around her unhappy.

Dolores, on the other hand, was a happy little song-bird. She loved music and she made everyone love her. Dolores had only one trouble and that was her sister, Felicia.

The strange part of this is that "felicia"

means happiness, and "dolores" means sorrow.

It so happened that when these twins were born, Señor Gallego had said to his wife, "Let us name them Dolores (sorrow) and Felicia (happiness). The sorrow is for our old home, our dear Mexico, which we have had to leave. The happiness is for our new home, the great United States where we find peace."

So that was how the dark, happy little girl came to be named "Sorrow"; and the blond, unhappy little girl, "Happiness."

Of course, Señor Gallego had not known then how the children were going to grow up. Then he had beheld a pretty blond baby and a dark sweet-faced baby together in their cradle.

The Gallego automobile drew up at the school entrance. Children were arriving in red and yellow costumes. There was much laughter and excitement.

Red and yellow banners waved in the breeze. Long tables were spread with red and yellow cloths.

As Dolores and Felicia stepped out of their car, the girls and boys stared at them. These twins were looked upon as something like princesses at the school.

Felicia always told many stories about her father's people who came from Mexico. Some of her stories were true.

The wealthy landowners of Mexico are descendants of Spanish nobles. They are still considered nobles. So proud Felicia believed herself to be a great lady.

But sometimes she went too far. Today was one of those times. Felicia was feeling very fine in her handsome costume. She was bragging to the other children and acting very important.

"Tomorrow I am going back to my palace in Mexico," she said grandly. "You know that my father is the King of Mexico!"

The teacher happened to be passing. She stopped.

"Felicia," asked the teacher, "what did I hear you say?"

The little girl grew fiery red and did not answer. A child beside her spoke up.

"Felicia told us that her father is the King of Mexico," said the child.

The teacher sat down among the children. She looked at Felicia sadly and shook her head.

"I am surprised, Felicia," she said, "that you do not know more about your father's country."

Still Felicia was silent. She was wishing she had not spoken that way.

The teacher went on, "It is strange that the daughter of a Mexican gentleman does not know that the last Mexican Emperor was Maximilian (măk′sĭ-mĭl′yăn). He was an Austrian archduke who only ruled a short time. Since then Mexico has been a republic, ruled by a president, like the United States."

"I do know that," murmured Felicia. Tears were starting to her eyes.

"Then why, my dear child, did you say that your father is the King?" asked the teacher.

"Because she is a big story-teller!" cried a boy in the group.

Felicia's eyes blazed, though they were full of tears.

"I am not!" she screamed.

"Come, children," spoke the teacher, "this is a feast day and we are meant to be happy. Let us forget this. When Felicia goes to Mexico, she will send us picture postcards of that beautiful land. I'm sure she will not tell untruths again. Will you, dear?"

She patted Felicia's hand kindly and left the group. She did not know what would happen as soon as her back was turned.

Felicia made a dash for the boy who had

HE PULLED OFF HER MANTILLA

called her a story-teller. She slapped his face hard. This made the boy furious and he pulled off her mantilla.

This so enraged Felicia that she began to scream and hit the boy with all her might. Soon there was a terrible battle going on.

Felicia was like a little wildcat. She had the boy on the ground and was pummeling him. Some of the children tried to stop her, but she was too strong.

The boy did not want to hit too hard for fear of hurting a girl. He knew that such an act would not be gentlemanly. But Felicia's blows were hurting him.

At last the teacher came and separated the two. Dolores ran up to her sister.

"Oh, Felicia," poor Dolores cried, "how could you!"

The teacher was examining the boy to see if he was badly hurt. Dolores threw her arm about Felicia and drew her toward a bench.

FELICIA WAS LIKE A LITTLE WILDCAT

"Oh, Felicia, your beautiful costume is ruined!" wailed Dolores.

She was right. The fine mantilla that had belonged to their grandmother was torn. The embroidered dress was soiled. Felicia did not look like a grand lady now. She looked very mussed-up and dirty.

"Now you will not win the prize!" moaned the sister.

SHE WAS ALWAYS SORRY IN THE END

"Well," snapped Felicia, "why are you crying about it? Maybe you'll be able to win it now!"

But unselfish Dolores had not thought of that. She was so proud of her pretty sister, and she loved to have her admired.

"Why must you always get into trouble, Felicia?" Dolores asked.

Then Felicia put her head on her sister's shoulder and sobbed. She could not help doing the foolish things she did.

She was just a very quick-tempered, spoiled little girl. But she was always sorry in the end.

CHAPTER VIII

MR. FIVE TOES

"How very hot it is!" complained Felicia.

"Well, anyway, it isn't raining any more," replied Dolores.

"Oh, I'm sick of this old trip!" Felicia sighed.

The Gallego family was on the train speeding through Mexico. The trip so far had been very tiresome.

"Don't be discouraged, girls," said their father. "Soon we'll arrive in the town of Chihuahua (chē-wä′wä). And you know what I promised there!"

Both girls smiled at their father's reminder.

Chihuahua was the first real Mexican city that they were to reach.

100

MR. FIVE TOES

On the trip it had rained. Mexican rains come in the summer. The winters there are like our summers.

But in this part of Mexico it was dry and hot. Mrs. Gallego had gone to bed with a headache.

"How long shall we stay in Chihuahua, daddy?" asked Felicia.

"Until we find Mr. Five Toes," replied her father.

"Mr. Five Toes?" inquired Dolores.

Felicia, too, looked puzzled.

"Yes," answered Señor Gallego, "the Chihuahua puppy I promised you."

"Yes, I know. But why 'Mr. Five Toes'?" asked Felicia.

"Oh, because all Chihuahua dogs have five little toes right together on each foot. Didn't you know that?" asked their father.

"Why, no," both girls answered at once.

"Well, it is true," said the Señor. "The real Chihuahua dogs are very fine indeed."

Dolores and Felicia could hardly wait to reach the city where they were to receive this wonderful present.

At last the train pulled into the station. The twins were not so interested in seeing their first Mexican city as they were in finding their promised dog.

"We must first go to the hotel and clean

up," Señor Gallego said. "Then off we go for Mr. Five Toes!"

After the family was settled in the hotel, Dolores and Felicia at last heard the happy words they had been awaiting.

Their father announced, "Come along now. We can go on our search for Five Toes. Mother is resting before dinner, and we'll take a walk around."

They passed a number of people on the streets selling the little dogs.

But Señor Gallego warned, "No, wait. We must not buy those. They are not the real kind."

He then told them that many people try to sell fake Chihuahua dogs. But he said that he could easily tell the difference between these and the real ones.

At last they found Five Toes. He had five little nails on each foot.

He was just a tiny thing. He weighed about three pounds.

"Why, he doesn't weigh as much as my big doll!" cried Dolores.

He was tan and had no hair. Sometimes these dogs are called Mexican Hairless. He had butterfly ears and lovely, sad eyes. The girls were wild with delight.

"Now, let us look around the city," said Señor Gallego. "Remember, this is your first glimpse of a Mexican town."

"Oh, I can't look at a thing but just this darling little Five Toes!" squealed Felicia.

But they did manage to see a part of Chihuahua. It is a city of factories and mills and the people seemed very busy.

Next morning the Gallego family set forth once more.

They were on their way to Mexico City where Señor Gallego had business which needed his attention.

But he also had important things to do in other cities before they reached the capital.

A place that the girls were not likely to

forget was Monterrey (mŏn'tĕr-rā'), meaning "king mountain."

The city is set in the midst of huge mountains. They are strangely barren mountains
and look very mysterious.

Then, Señor Gallego took them on a drive
to see the Garcia (gär-thē'ä) Caves near
Monterrey. They were led through many
different caverns, strange and mysterious.

One cavern is called the Chamber of the
Bells. If you strike any part of that cave,
the silvery sound of a bell rings out.

There are caves called the Bishop's Palace, the Chamber of the White Lake, and
the Girl's Room, a dainty cave of pink and
white. There is the Room of the Broken
Heart where a huge stone heart hangs down
from the ceiling.

They wanted to explore further but Señor
Gallego thought it time to leave.

"The cave goes on and on," he exclaimed.
"No one has yet found the end."

From Monterrey they journeyed to San Luis Potosi (sän lŏo-ēs′ po′to-sē′). The Gallego girls were delighted as they walked through the quaint streets and saw the Indians selling their wares.

They saw large oxcarts laden with sugar cones. They saw the slow donkey boys lazily selling water.

They tasted a new fruit, chirimoyas (chĭr′ĭ-moi′äz). They are custard apples and taste like pineapple custard.

After that interesting visit they began their trip to Guanajuato (gwä′nä-hwä′tō). This town is off the main line of travel to Mexico City but Señor Gallego had to go there on business. The girls were glad, for they were charmed with this old Mexican town.

"My goodness!" exclaimed Dolores, "It looks like a toy village."

"It looks like a lot of baby blocks piled on top of each other," cried Felicia.

GUANAJUATO LOOKS LIKE A TOY VILLAGE

That is really what it did resemble. For Guanajuato is built between hills, and the pink and blue and yellow and green houses seem to stand on each other's heads.

They walked to their hotel. The narrow street twisted and turned.

"One almost has to be a snake to get along these winding streets," laughed Señor Gallego.

"Or a mountain goat," panted Dolores, "to climb these hills!"

They rested in Guanajuato only over night. But Dolores and Felicia felt sorry to leave the pretty town.

"Those little houses look as though they were just hanging onto the cliffs," remarked Dolores as their train pulled out of the station.

"Yes," agreed Felicia, "and if you gave them a good push they'd fall all in a heap on top of one another!"

"Well," laughed their father, "it's a good

751. Front of Theatre Juarez Guanajuato Mex.   Waite Photo.

THEATRE JUAREZ, GUANAJUATO

thing we are not staying here or I'm afraid my Felicia might try it. And then, good-bye, Guanajuato!"

Mrs. Gallego was glad to leave behind the hilly town. She was not a good climber.

"I am glad that we are on our way to a large city at last. I do not like going through these small towns," sighed the girls' mother.

"Why, mother?" asked Felicia.

"Because—" Mrs. Gallego stopped. She started to say, "Because one hears so much about bandits and train robberies in Mexico."

But she thought it best not to frighten the girls.

So she said, "Oh, I'm so anxious to reach Guadalajara (gwä′thä-lä-hä′rä). To me it is the most beautiful city in Mexico."

"To me it is beautiful because you were born there, my dear," said Señor Gallego to his wife.

But even for those who were not born there, Guadalajara has a charm. The girls were looking forward to seeing the city they had heard their mother talk so much about.

After Mexico City and their own hacienda, Guadalajara interested them most in this new land.

CHAPTER IX

ON THE WAY TO MEXICO CITY

"Here we are in the city of beautiful women!" exclaimed Señor Gallego.

They were driving through Guadalajara.

"That must be true," agreed Dolores, "for mother was born here."

Mrs. Gallego blushed.

Guadalajara is really noted for its pretty girls. It is like a Spanish city. It was even named after a city in Spain. The word means rocky river.

The weather in Guadalajara is so mild that the people hardly know when winter comes.

The girls were interested in the large sombreros worn by most of the men.

"I must tell you a funny story about those

112

SPANISH MEXICAN GIRLS

hats," said Mother Gallego. "At one time the men of Guadalajara tried to see how wide they could make their hat brims.

"Each man wanted to outdo the other, until the large hats became a real nuisance. They bothered people in the streets; they could hardly be pushed through doorways; they were just terrible!

"So at last the law made the men pay a tax on all hats over a certain size. That stopped the foolish fashion."

They noticed that the city was beautifully clean.

"I never thought Mexican cities were so clean," said Felicia approvingly.

"Shame, child!" scolded her father. "Why, the old Mexicans were perhaps the cleanest people in the world. You have heard of the Mayas (mä′yäz) of Yucatan, haven't you?"

"No," answered Felicia. "Where is Yucatan?"

"It is at the southeast end of Mexico,"

replied her father. "It is the place where many valuable ruins were dug up. Long before your California was even thought of, these Mayas of Yucatan were living in splendor.

"It seems that there was an old Spanish law which made it right for any man to beat his wife if she did not have his bath awaiting him every day."

"Oh, dear," cried Mother Gallego, "as soon as we reach the hotel I must prepare your bath, my king!"

The girls laughed.

As they drove on they noticed little desks set right out on the sidewalks. At these desks were men who were writing letters for people who cannot read and write. They are called "letter writers" and they make their living this way.

The Gallego family spent many happy days in Guadalajara. Mother Gallego knew many people and they had a gay time. They

Photo by Underwood & Underwood

WRITING LETTERS FOR PEOPLE WHO CANNOT READ
AND WRITE

had a better time than most travelers would have had, for they could speak Spanish.

They left Guadalajara with regret.

"I'm going to miss the ringing of the church bells," sighed Dolores.

"I still hear the sound," said Felicia. "I think they must have thousands of churches in Guadalajara."

They were again on the train. At last they were on their way to Mexico City and their own hacienda.

At one of the stations were two blind musicians who played their guitars under the train windows. People said that they had been doing this for many, many years.

"Think of all the trainloads of people those poor blind men must have sung to!" exclaimed Dolores.

At every station the Indians tried to sell the travelers fruit and candy and hot Mexican food.

"How can the people keep eating those hot

81 Making the Mexican drawn work

Waite Photo

MAKING MEXICAN DRAWNWORK

peppery things and still live?" asked Felicia shuddering.

Her father answered, "They do not live long. The rich people of Mexico eat far too much and they become ill. Of course the poor people cannot afford to do that. They live on corn and beans and things like that which are really wholesome."

Señor Gallego bought some tortillas and started to eat.

Suddenly Dolores screamed, "Oh, look! Mr. Five Toes likes tortillas, too!"

The tiny dog was trying to take a bite out of the Señor's tortilla.

"He's a true Mexican," laughed the girls' father.

He gave the puppy a piece of the pancake. Five Toes gobbled it up and looked for more.

The train stopped for a short time at the station of Querétaro (kā-rā'tä-rō).

"Here is an old historical city," explained Señor Gallego. "You would not think that

A MEXICAN MOUNTAIN VILLAGE

a sleepy little town like this could have been so important. But it is the spot where Maximilian, Mexico's last Emperor, was defeated.

"It was this town that saw the last of Mexico's monarchy."

"What is a monarchy?" asked Felicia.

"A monarchy is a kingdom," answered her father.

Felicia was silent. She was thinking of her foolish remark at school that day.

Men selling opals shouted through the windows of their train. Felicia begged for some of the pretty gems. Señor Gallego bought a few.

Querétaro looked like a city in the very old world. It might have been a city in the Holy Land. It certainly did not seem to the travelers that they were in America.

And now, let us leave the Gallego family flying along in the fast train toward Mexico City. Let us leave them and go back to Dodo.

CHAPTER X

THE BULLFIGHT

Dodo, too, was on his way to Mexico City. But he was not flying along in a fast train. Dodo was jogging along on a slow gray donkey. His eyes were closed.

Dodo had helped the other boy to carry his jars to market. He had then promised the boy to send the money for the little donkey. He had said, "goodbye," mounted the donkey, and started on his way to Mexico City.

The little gray donkey seemed to like Dodo from the first. He did not object to carrying the boy. Dodo did not prod him nor shout at him. Dodo was content to jog peacefully along.

He called the little animal "Amigo" (ä-

HE WENT FAST ASLEEP

mē′gō), which means friend in Spanish.

Dodo trusted his new friend so much that he went fast asleep on his back while they moved along. But all at once Amigo stopped. Dodo awoke, but he did not open his eyes. He kicked Amigo lightly. But Amigo refused to move.

Dodo kicked a little harder. Still the animal stood motionless.

"Go along!" said Dodo sleepily. His eyes were still closed.

Amigo did not move.

"Lazy Amigo!" growled Dodo, forgetting how lazy he himself was. "Why do you stop?"

But when Dodo opened his eyes and saw where he was he did not scold Amigo any more. For Dodo saw that Amigo had stopped right on the edge of a deep ditch. He looked down and saw how very far it was to the bottom. Then he looked about him. They had strayed off the road and were in a wild part of the country.

Dodo said, "You have lost the way while I slept. But you are a good little donkey for you disobeyed me when I urged you on. If you had gone further we should have gone into the ditch."

He turned Amigo around and started to

look for the main road. He soon found it and they jogged on.

At last they entered Mexico City. They stopped at an inn, just outside the city. They rode into a court behind the inn. Here Dodo found a boy who was working for the inn-keeper.

"Will you keep my donkey here for me while I go to the city?" asked Dodo.

The boy promised to care for Amigo, and Dodo gave him a coin. Then he walked straight to the bull-ring.

The bullfight arena was crowded with people all anxious to see the cruel sport. A military band was playing. It was all very gay.

Dodo had just enough money for his ticket. He sat down on a bench among the noisy crowd.

A bald-headed man sat in front of Dodo. All at once a juicy orange hit the bald-headed man. Squash!

The bald-headed man looked around. He

was very angry. Again, squash! Another
soft orange on his bald head. He stood up
and began to shout and wave his arms.

The crowd was laughing. Dodo thought
it great fun. He thought he would like bullfights.

Then the real show began. The bald-
headed man sat down and the people forgot
him. They all looked at the ring.

The bullfighters were dressed in tight-fit-
ting uniforms covered with silver embroid-
ery. Dodo's eyes grew bright.

Suddenly the crowd exclaimed, "Ah, el
toro (ĕl tō′rō)!"

"Toro" means bull. The bull rushed in.
His horns were long and pointed.

One of the bullfighters waved a red cloak
before the bull. This made the animal very
angry. Bulls do not like the color red.

Some of the bullfighters sat upon horses.
They held long pikes with steel points at the
ends of them.

THE BULLFIGHT ARENA WAS CROWDED WITH PEOPLE

The bull trotted over to one of these horsemen. Then Dodo saw that the horses were blindfolded.

"Why?" he asked himself.

It seemed very unfair. There was great danger for these horses. Surely the fighters should give them a chance to see and to protect themselves. But instead, they blindfolded them.

Poor Dodo did not know yet that the bullfight is the most unfair and most cruel sport that exists. But he was soon to find this out.

While Dodo was watching the bullfight, Señor Gallego was entering the same arena. Señor Gallego was entering with Manuel.

Señor Gallego had arrived in Mexico City with his family, and Manuel had met them at the train.

The family was settled at a hotel. Now the father of the girls was going to the bullfight with Manuel.

You may think that Señor Gallego and Manuel were cruel men to like bullfights. But you know what a kind father the Señor really was. You know, too, how good Manuel had been to Dodo even if Dodo did not belong to Manuel.

Many men who cheer at these horrible fights are not bad men at all. It is a strange thing.

The fight continued. It grew very exciting. The bull was teased without mercy. He was so angry that he rushed at the men. But the men protected themselves.

It was the poor horses that could not see to dodge the bull. Many horses are killed every year at bullfights in Mexico.

"What is that?" asked Señor Gallego.

A crowd had gathered in the corner of the ring. A group of men surrounded some one who was shouting.

"Let us go and see," said Manuel.

They found the crowd surrounding a boy

who was trying to run into the ring and seemed terribly upset. Some of the men were holding the boy who struggled to get loose.

"Let me go!" screamed the boy, "I will do it again. It is not fair! Let me go!"

"What is the trouble?" asked Manuel.

One of the crowd answered, "That boy ran into the ring and lifted the bandage from a horse's eyes. They will arrest him."

Manuel and Señor Gallego pushed closer. They saw the boy struggling and trying to break loose.

"I shall take off all the bandages from their eyes," he was crying. "They must see the danger!"

Manuel looked closely at the boy. It was Dodo.

"Dodo!" Manuel exclaimed. He rushed over to Dodo.

"Ah, Manuel," cried poor Dodo, "they will not take off the bandages. It is so terrible!"

AIR VIEW OF MEXICO CITY

Courtesy of Missouri Pacific Co.

Manuel saw that the boy was in a state of great distress. Dodo could not bear to see animals tortured. He thought of his little donkey. These poor horses in the ring did not have a chance.

"Come along," said Manuel. "Come away, Dodo, outside."

Together Señor Gallego and Manuel led the boy out of the arena. They drove him to Señor Gallego's hotel.

As they drove, Manuel told the boy's story to the Señor. He told him how Dodo had run away because he did not want to be a mozo.

Just then they stopped in front of the hotel. Dodo did not want to be taken into the beautiful rooms of the Señor's family. He wanted to go back to his little donkey.

He did not like the way the Señor's wife looked at him. She was dressed in a silk gown trimmed with shining things. He was afraid of these wealthy people from the United States.

The little girl with golden curls stared. It made him drop his eyes to the floor.

But the little dark girl looked kind. She was the only one who smiled—the only one besides Señor Gallego.

That gentleman turned to his daughters.

"Wouldn't you like Dodo to come back to the hacienda with us?" he asked.

The girls did not answer, but Dolores smiled shyly.

Manuel broke in, "Si, Señor," he said, "if the young ladies wish to have Dodo for their mozo he shall come."

"Oh, that would be nice," said Felicia, looking pleased. "I should like to have a little boy waiting upon me. I should feel like a princess!"

Manuel smiled and thought what a beautiful princess Felicia would make. But Dodo's heart sank very low.

"Perhaps he would not like that at all," Dolores spoke up.

"Ah, if the Señoritas wish it," said Manuel, "then it does not matter whether Dodo likes it or not."

Manuel looked up to this family as if they really ruled over him.

But Dodo was burning with fury. He had not yet recovered from that terrible bull-fight. Now he felt like one of those blind-folded horses. Trapped! A mozo! Oh, there must be some way of escape!

"I shall take Dodo out now," Manuel announced. "We shall have our dinner and find a room for the night. Tomorrow, Señor, do we leave for the hacienda?"

"No, Manuel," answered Señor Gallego. "My daughters are anxious to see Mexico City. So we shall stay here a few days before going home to the hacienda."

Manuel offered, "Perhaps Dodo and I might take the Señoritas around the city tomorrow? Perhaps we might show them the sights?"

THE CATHEDRAL. CITY OF MEXICO

"An excellent idea," agreed the Señor.

But Dodo did not think the idea excellent at all. It made him shudder to think of being all day with those two unpleasant girls.

No, both girls were not unpleasant. Not the little dark one. The little dark one had good things in her eyes.

CHAPTER XI

CITY OF MEXICO

The next morning Dolores and Felicia had an early breakfast. They had spiced chocolate and sweet rolls for breakfast.

This may seem a strange morning meal. But it did not seem at all strange to Dolores and Felicia.

They always drank chocolate and ate sweet rolls for breakfast. That was because their parents came from Mexico.

Manuel called for them early. Dodo was with him looking very unhappy.

The four started their tour of the oldest city in the western hemisphere. What an interesting city it is! It is modern, yet very old-fashioned. It is magnificent, yet full of misery.

1680. Mexican Gentleman in Charro suit.   Waite. Photo.

A MEXICAN GENTLEMAN RIDING IN THE PASEO

The Paseo de la Reforma (pä-sā′ō de lä rā-fōr′mä) is one of the most beautiful drives in the world. Yet not far from this magnificent street are poor, dirty little alleys where people live in misery.

Automobiles fill the avenues. Airplanes fly overhead. Fashionable shops line the boulevards. Newsboys shout. Bright Spanish signs glitter. Chewing gum and American candy for sale! Everything like a modern city.

But then, all at once a string of donkeys passes. They carry loads upon their backs. All traffic stops to let them through. Imagine a thing like that happening in New York, Chicago, Los Angeles, Boston, or any other big city in the United States!

Women sit upon the ground in the market place. They sell fruits and toys and such glorious flowers.

Men with gay-colored blankets and wide hats walk by carrying baskets on their

Photo by Ewing Galloway, N. Y.

PACK MULE TRAIN IN A PUBLIC SQUARE

heads—everything like a very lazy, old-fashioned city.

The girls gazed in wonder at the Cathedral which faces the Plaza. It is one of the largest churches in the world. It is built in the form of a Greek cross.

Many old buildings in this city are slowly sinking into the ground. The Cathedral is one of them.

But some of the people believe that the great building is swung on giant chains. They believe that it can never be shaken down.

For in Mexico there are earthquakes often. The earth trembles and sometimes houses fall down.

Manuel and the two girls and Dodo walked down funny narrow streets and pretty wide avenues.

The streets have queer names. They have Spanish names that mean such things as Lost Child, Walking Priest, and Sad Indian.

Photo by Ewing Galloway, N. Y.

THE ART OF BASKET MAKING IN MEXICO

They drove out to Chapultepec (chä-pōol′ tā-pĕk′) Park where the President of Mexico lives. They could see in the distance the two great volcanoes, or fire mountains.

Years ago these volcanoes sent up smoke and fire. But now they are just like other mountains.

Their names are Popocatepetl (pō-pō′kä-tā′pĕt'l) and Ixtaccihuatl (ēs′täk-sē′hwät'l). These names are very hard for us to say. But they mean Smoky Mountain and White Woman in the Aztec Indian language.

Ixtaccihuatl is shaped like a sleeping woman. They say that she is the wife of Popocatepetl, which they call "Popo" for short. The Floating Gardens are one of the loveliest spots in Mexico. They lie a short way from the city. Years ago the gardens really floated. But today they do not move.

The flower beds are still separated by narrow streams. Boats glide lazily among poppies, and roses, and lilies.

Manuel took the girls and Dodo for a ride in one of the boats.

"Would you like to hear how these gardens first started?" asked Manuel.

The girls were interested.

"Yes, please tell us," they said.

"At one time," began Manuel, "certain Indians were driven here and could not leave. This was then a great lake.

"These Indians could not live without their corn. So they tangled together some of these water plants and sprinkled earth upon them. Then they planted their corn.

"Gradually, the Indians' vegetable garden grew to be a flower garden as well. Today, most of the flowers sold in Mexico City come from here."

"Oh, it is beautiful! What a fine story!" cried Dolores.

"The flowers smell so sweet," said Felicia, "that I don't ever want to leave."

Manuel smiled.

THE FLOATING GARDENS

"But we must go," he answered. "I want to show you the Porcelain Palace."

"What is that?" asked Felicia.

"It is a very old palace made of porcelain, or tiles," Manuel explained.

"Tiles?" inquired Felicia, surprised. "Like a bathroom?"

Manuel did not understand just why both girls had to laugh. But then, Manuel did not have a tiled bathroom in his hut.

"There is a story about the Porcelain Palace," said Manuel.

"Oh, then let us go and see it at once!" cried Felicia.

She nearly tipped the boat over in her eagerness. Dolores screamed. Manuel scolded and frowned.

Dodo thought, "She is like a cat. She is too quick."

Dodo feared Felicia as he might have feared a young tigress. But it was different with Dolores.

On the way to the Porcelain Palace Dolores tried to make Dodo talk to her. But
the boy was strangely quiet and thoughtful.
Dodo had his own thoughts. He was plan-
ning.

The Porcelain Palace was really made of
blue and white tiles. But it was very dirty
with age. A modern café has been built
there. Manuel told the story of the palace.

"In olden days," said Manuel, "there lived
a young man who was fond of spending
much money. When he had spent all his
money he went to his father and asked for
more.

"His father refused. Then he told his son
the old proverb which says, 'Those who
spend much money shall never build porcelain palaces.'"

"How silly!" scoffed Felicia.

But she said it in English and Manuel did
not understand. Dolores gave her a cross
look.

Manuel continued, "Then the father sent his son away from home. The young man was angry and did not forget what his father had said. He determined to be more careful and to save his money.

"One day he became so rich that he built this Porcelain Palace. He did it to show his father that spendthrifts can build porcelain palaces after all."

The girls had been listening attentively to the story. So they did not see what Dodo had done.

Dodo had been stealing quietly away.

When they looked around after the story was finished the boy was gone.

"Where is Dodo?" asked Felicia.

Both girls looked questioningly at Manuel.

Manuel stood up and frowned.

"He has run away," said Manuel. "He is a strange niño. He does not want to go back to the hacienda and serve the Señoritas."

Dolores answered firmly, "I don't blame

him a bit. He does not want to wait upon two strange girls. He wants to be free."

Felicia tossed her head.

"He should be glad to serve us!" she said.

Manuel did not speak. He was wondering where poor Dodo had gone.

CHAPTER XII

"YOU MUST GO!"

Dodo's first thought was for his donkey. He hurried to the inn where he had left the animal. The donkey was delighted to see his young master. He put his soft, velvet nose in Dodo's hand.

"Poor Amigo!" said Dodo. "Did you miss me?"

Then Dodo hugged the soft gray head and thought of Amigo's cousins, those poor horses who were abused in the bull ring.

"They shall never abuse you, Amigo," he said to the little donkey. "You are my friend."

Dodo mounted the donkey, lazily closed his eyes, and rode along. He had determined to escape from Manuel and these strangers.

"THEY SHALL NEVER ABUSE YOU, AMIGO"

He feared the little blond girl who moved like a cat and tossed her head like a princess. He felt that never could he go back to the hacienda and work for her.

But once again Dodo was between the

frying pan and the fire. It would be impossible for him to go back to the unfair potter. It would be even more impossible for him to be a bullfighter. He shuddered as he thought of that.

Oh, if only he might just ride along like this forever and never worry about anything! But he knew that this could not be. He must find a place to sleep and food to eat. He must, besides, earn money to pay the boy who had sold him his donkey.

Why not try another potter? Perhaps he might find one who would treat him kindly.

Dodo jogged on.

When night came he curled up by the side of the road and slept. Next morning he begged breakfast at a farmhouse.

Thus on he rode.

He passed fields of sugar cane.

He came to a rock upon which strange pictures had been carved. He stopped. The carving interested him. But he did not know that these pictures had been carved hundreds and hundreds of years ago.

They made him think once more of painting and modeling. So he urged the donkey on until he came to a potter's home outside a small village.

The potter's wife was kind and gave him tortillas. There were many small brown children about the potter's house. They made him think of Manuel's children. Suddenly he felt homesick.

But when the potter came home, Dodo said to him, "I should like to stay and learn your trade."

But he did not mention anything about being a mozo.

"What will you do for me if I teach you my trade?" asked the potter.

Dodo did not want to do anything.

However, he knew that he could not say this to the potter.

So he answered, "I shall do what you tell

me to do. But I must earn some money."

"Aha," the potter laughed, "you wish me to pay you for being my pupil?"

"No," replied Dodo. "I only ask to work for you until I can make enough to pay for my donkey. Then I shall learn your trade."

The potter stroked his chin. He looked at Dodo's donkey.

"Very well," he said. "You shall be a water-carrier. And you shall pay me part of what you earn. Then I can keep you here."

Dodo was pleased and he stayed with the potter.

Every day he harnessed Amigo. Great red water jugs hung on either side of the animal's back. Then Dodo led Amigo to a public fountain.

He filled the water jugs with cool mountain water and peddled this water from house to house. Donkeys have been called "the water-works of Mexico."

All day long and every day Dodo worked. The money he made he brought home.

But this potter was a fair man. He took half of Dodo's earnings and let the boy keep the other half.

Soon Dodo had enough to pay for his donkey. He sent the money to the other boy.

Then he said to the potter, "Now I need not work as a water-carrier any more. Now I should like to learn your trade."

But the potter shook his head.

"That cannot be," he said. "You cannot stop working. You must continue being a water-carrier. You must bring me money each day. Otherwise I cannot keep you here. I am a poor man."

Dodo was heartbroken.

He was very tired of peddling water. He wanted to rest. He wanted to model in clay and paint.

But what could he do?

So he said, "Very well. If you will teach

me to model and paint each evening, I shall be a water-carrier by day."

The potter agreed to this plan. When he saw what splendid work Dodo could do with the clay and the brush, he was indeed surprised. But this did not last long.

One day Dodo came home without money.

The potter asked, "Where is the money for the water?"

Dodo said, "I did not peddle water today. I painted this vase."

He held up a little vase upon which he had painted the picture of his donkey.

The potter said, "That is well done. But you must not do it again when you should be working."

"I do not like to work," said Dodo.

The potter stroked his chin as he had done that first day.

He replied, "But you must work or I cannot keep you here. I have enough jars and vases to sell without adding yours. And, besides, that is my work. I cannot be expected to go out and peddle water while you sit home and paint. Can I?"

Dodo shook his head sadly. But he grew lazier all the time. He hardly ever peddled water any more. He slept most of the day when he was not modeling and painting.

One day he lay on his stomach under a tree with a clump of clay in his hands. He was feeling very dreamy. He was thinking of that day when he had run away from Mexico City, and from Manuel and those two little girls.

The little dark girl had really been kind. Dodo began to wonder if it might not be pleasant after all to be the mozo of that sweet little girl.

He could see her smiling face before him. All at once his hands began to shape a model of her face in clay. He finished working. He had made a clay image of Dolores.

The potter came and found him lying un-

HE WAS FEELING VERY DREAMY

der a tree. The potter was very angry.

"I have been kind to you," said the potter. "And I have been patient. But you are a lazy boy. Therefore, I cannot keep you here. You must go."

Dodo lifted his dark eyes to the potter's face.

"See," he said. He held up the clay image of Dolores.

The potter took it in his hands. He looked at it for a long time. Then he gave it back to Dodo and he shook his head.

"It is a great shame," the potter said slowly, "a great shame."

"What is a shame?" asked Dodo.

The potter answered, "You are a very clever artist. You could make something of your life. But you never will because you are too lazy. I should be glad to teach you all I know, and help you, if you would only work. But, if you do not work, you cannot expect to succeed."

"But I do not like to work," Dodo said. "Work is not fun."

"No, it is not fun," agreed the potter. "Neither is it fun for me to keep you here. Tomorrow you go."

So the next day Dodo left the potter's house.

CHAPTER XIII

HACIENDA GALLEGO

The Gallego hacienda was almost like a little village. Many people lived on it. These many people were Indian peons. They tended the cattle and helped to keep the Gallego hacienda in good condition.

Manuel was the head of the hacienda. Señor Gallego liked and trusted Manuel. As we know, he had his own hut on the great ranch. It was the hut where Dodo had lived.

Today all the Indians on the place were trying to catch a glimpse of the Señor Gallego and his family. They knew that the owners of the hacienda were arriving.

The Señor himself had come often before to the hacienda. But this was the first time he had brought his children.

WORKMEN ON A HACIENDA

"Oh, daddy," squealed the two girls as they drove into the large ranch, "is this really all ours?"

"Yes, chicks," said Señor Gallego. "What's the matter? Don't you like our little garden?"

"Our little garden?" breathed Felicia. "Why, it's a regular kingdom!"

Felicia was seeing herself sitting upon a throne, ruling over all the vast country she saw before her—over all the brown people dressed in white with straw hats on their heads.

They saw that the hacienda was surrounded by tall, prickly cactuses.

"It looks like—" began Dolores. Then she wrinkled her brow thoughtfully. "What does it look like?" she puzzled.

"Like a great organ," her father remarked, "Isn't that what you thought?"

"Yes, that's it," the little girl assented. "A big pipe organ."

PICKING TOMATOES ON A HACIENDA

"And that is just what this kind of cactus is called, too," Señor Gallego explained. "It is called Organ Cactus."

"It makes a fine fence," observed Felicia. "And it keeps everyone out!"

The Señor laughed.

"You are right," he agreed. "It does."

They passed a tiny church.

"That belongs to us, too," Mother Gallego said.

"Our own church!" marveled Felicia.

They were now approaching Manuel's little hut.

Señor Gallego decided to tease Felicia. He had a twinkle in his eye. He pointed to Manuel's hut.

He said, "And that is our house!"

He watched Felicia's face.

"Our house?" she cried. "Oh, daddy, not the house where we are to live! Why, I thought it was a palace on a hill! Oh, I thought—"

Photo by Ewing Galloway, N. Y.

COFFEE PICKERS IN MEXICO

The words choked her. She was about to cry.

But they drove right past Manuel's hut and did not stop.

Felicia looked at her father. He was trying not to burst into laughter.

"Daddy!" scolded Felicia, "you were teasing me!"

Soon Felicia found out how much daddy had really been teasing. For when they drew up in front of their real house, even Felicia could not have asked for a more splendid castle.

In the outer court sat some peons playing musical instruments. They were welcoming the Señor and his family. Beneath a window sat a little girl playing on the Mexican harp.

Music—beauty everywhere!

The two girls could hardly wait to explore the beautiful Spanish mansion.

They found a patio (pät′yō), or inner

PLAYING ON THE MEXICAN HARP

court, filled with trees and flowers and a fountain. Every Spanish and Mexican house is built around a patio.

They ran up the stone stairway to the flat roof. This roof is where the family would spend much time. It was furnished with swings and comfortable chairs.

It was so high up that Felicia exclaimed, "We can look down and see the whole world, Dolores!"

Dolores was speechless.

Below them lay their own hacienda, their kingdom. Surrounding them were great mountains. Fields of giant plants stretched away to meet the mountains.

They were the famous maguey (măg′wā) plants. The maguey is like a magic grab bag to the Mexicans. They use every part of the plant.

Sometimes they cook the roots for food.

They shingle their houses with its dried leaves.

MUSIC EVERYWHERE

They make cotton, twine, rope and paper from the fibre of the leaves.

They braid the rope into mats to use for beds and chairs.

Sometimes the magic grab bag is called the Needle and Thread Plant. This is because one may pull out a long spike like a needle and push it into the plant.

When it comes out again it is really threaded with little fibres like thread.

The most important gift to the Mexicans from the maguey plant is its honey water. They make this into their favorite drink which they call pulque (pool′kā).

But the funniest thing of all is that even the maguey worm is cooked and eaten and considered a very fine food.

The girls stood on their roof and looked over the countryside.

A mozo dressed in white appeared before them.

"Dinner is served, niñas," he said.

A FIELD OF MAGUEY PLANTS

All the Indian servants call their mistresses "niña." No matter how old a lady might be, she is "niña," or "little one," to her Mexican servant.

"Gracious," cried Dolores, "is it that late already?"

The mozo told them it was nineteen o'clock. That meant seven o'clock the way we tell time. But in Mexico it is different.

For many days the girls wandered happily about the house and gardens.

Their father gave them two sturdy ponies. They rode all around the hacienda.

But at last one day Mrs. Gallego said, "Now it is time to give up some of your play. You must give some time to work."

"Oh, dear," sighed Felicia, "why must we work in the summer time?"

"Because, you know," her mother replied, "the old saying goes, 'all play and no work makes Jack a dull boy!'"

Felicia tossed her head.

"Well, my name's not Jack. And I'm not a boy!" she answered rudely.

Mrs. Gallego looked sternly at her little daughter. Then she said, "Felicia, you must begin to learn to control your temper. Go into your room and stay there all afternoon."

Dolores felt sorry for Felicia. But she knew that her mother was right. Felicia must be punished.

Dolores practiced her music with the governess that afternoon. Her mother had given her the choice of lessons or music.

Dolores loved music. So she really did not mind singing songs and playing piano in the large, cool drawing room.

But the next day when Felicia was to join them, the stubborn girl refused.

"I won't play the old thing!" she cried. She threw her pretty guitar across the room.

Mrs. Gallego liked the girls to sing and play together.

"I WON'T PLAY THE OLD THING"

Dolores had a sweet voice and Felicia could play the guitar.

They had appeared at several charity affairs in Los Angeles. Everyone had admired the two pretty sisters. Felicia was a very musical child. The teacher had told Mrs. Gallego that Felicia had learned to play the guitar more quickly than any of her other pupils.

Also, Felicia loved music. But she did not love to practice.

Now she could not see why her vacation was to be spoiled by practice and work.

"This is stupid and I won't do it!" she repeated angrily.

Dolores watched her sister as she flounced out of the room in a rage.

"Now mother will punish her again," sighed Dolores.

But this time Mrs. Gallego turned Felicia over to the Señor.

The Señor met his little daughter in the sunny patio. He wore his Charro (chär'rō) suit. This is a very handsome costume that all Mexican gentlemen wear when they are living on their haciendas.

The Señor looked very tall and Felicia looked very small.

Felicia's father took both of her hands in his and asked kindly, "My dear little daughter, why don't you want to practice?"

Felicia pouted and replied, "Because it is work. And I hate work."

"Didn't you know that princesses have to work?" asked Señor Gallego.

Felicia looked interested.

"Yes, indeed," her father went on, "princesses have to learn even more than just ordinary little girls."

So Felicia decided to practice with the governess and Dolores each day.

But this did not last long.

One day she was nowhere to be found when it was lesson time.

Just before dinner she dashed into the house, dirty and mussed.

"Where have you been, Felicia?" asked Dolores.

WORKMEN'S QUARTERS ON A HACIENDA

Felicia sank breathlessly into a chair.

After a moment's rest, she told her story to Dolores.

"I got so tired of sitting around here," she began, "and I wanted to show myself to our subjects—"

"Our subjects?" interrupted Dolores.

"Yes, the Indians on the hacienda. The people we rule," answered her sister.

"Why, Felicia, you know we don't rule!" Dolores gasped.

Felicia ignored her sister's remark.

"Well, I went to that little hut," she continued, "And I saw some very dirty children there. They stared at me. And they did not bow down to me, or—or anything."

She paused to see how Dolores would take this news. But Dolores' eyes looked half sad and half angry. And she said nothing.

"So I just made them bow!" finished Felicia triumphantly.

"You what?" exclaimed Dolores.

A FAMILY OF PEONS AT HOME

"I rubbed their heads in the dirt!" said Felicia proudly.

"Felicia Gallego!" cried Dolores.

"But then," the little princess continued, "one of those horrid Indians began to fight me—"

Dolores shuddered. "Oh, dear," she sighed. "Do you mean you fought with one of daddy's own peons, right here on our own hacienda?"

Felicia smiled.

"Yes, of course," she replied. "And I showed him, too! His mother came out and made him pick up my hat. She called me a 'precious niña' and scolded the boy."

Felicia was very pleased with herself and didn't seem to mind her terrible actions.

But later Señor Gallego summoned Felicia into the patio once again. This time the father was not so gentle.

"Felicia," he said, "I told you once that I wished you to practice in the afternoons

"WHY HAVE YOU DISOBEYED ME?"

with your sister. Why have you disobeyed me?"

Felicia answered, "I don't like to work. It is no fun."

Señor Gallego frowned.

"No," he said. "But then, it sometimes keeps very stupid people out of trouble."

Felicia flushed. But she clenched her fists together.

"I have never before heard of a princess who fights," her father continued. "In fact, I never have heard of a real lady who fights. It is a boy's sport. And so, my dear Felicia, I am afraid I must give you a boy's punishment."

Felicia began to feel afraid.

She lifted her beautiful brown eyes to her father's face. He looked very serious, very severe.

"This will not be fun for me, Felicia," said Señor Gallego. "But I must do it anyway. Perhaps you will learn that everything we do need not be fun. Perhaps you will learn to be a lady. For I am afraid you can never be a princess."

Felicia was very frightened now. She had never seen her father this way before.

Señor Gallego went on talking.

"Princesses do not treat people the way

you treated those Indians today," he said. "Remember, they are not slaves. They are as free as you are. And they are much better behaved than you are, too.

"Furthermore, only those who act as ladies and gentlemen may live in this house. Therefore, you must go, Felicia."

Felicia's heart pounded. She caught her breath.

"What are you going to do, daddy?" asked the little girl, trembling. "Where must I go?"

"You will see," he answered firmly. "Come here to me tomorrow morning. Bring with you what you will need for a short trip. And now you may go to bed."

Felicia could hardly walk upstairs.

Her legs felt very weak.

CHAPTER XIV

FELICIA AND DODO

The next morning a very pale Felicia stood before her father. She wore her hat and carried a little traveling bag.

"I see that you are ready to go," said the Señor. "That is good. Now I shall take you to your new home."

Poor Felicia!

Señor Gallego had made up his mind to punish her so that she should learn a lesson.

He had told his wife about his plan. The good lady had at first objected. But the Señor had talked on and on.

"It is the only thing to do," he had said to his wife. "It will not hurt Felicia. I mean to leave her there until she appreciates her good fortune."

"I SEE THAT YOU ARE READY TO GO"

"But," the mother had objected, "she will be so unhappy in that tiny, dirty hut!"

"It is not dirty at all," Señor Gallego had corrected her. "I know Manuel's wife. She is a good mother. I do not fear leaving my child in her care.

"Felicia, of course, will not enjoy sleeping

on the floor and eating tortillas and beans. But it will not hurt her. And it is what she needs."

So Mrs. Gallego finally agreed to the plan.

The Señor promised to speak to Manuel's wife. He promised to tell Manuel's wife to watch over Felicia carefully.

Of course, Felicia must not know this. The Señor's daughter must be made to live like one of Manuel's own children.

"You must give her nothing that your own children do not have," said the Señor to Manuel's wife. "And she must learn to work. I hope that will teach her the lesson she needs."

So Felicia went to live in the little hut with Manuel's family.

The poor child cried herself to sleep that first night. She was rolled up in a blanket. She slept upon the floor. But she did not know that Manuel's wife was watching over her and feeling very sorry for her.

Dolores, in her comfortable bed at home, could not sleep. The little girl's heart was nearly breaking at her twin's sad plight.

Dolores was not allowed to see Felicia.

Felicia was not allowed to come home until her father gave her permission. The first morning in the hut was very strange to Felicia. Manuel's wife tried to teach her to sweep. But she refused to be taught.

The Indian woman then showed her how to make tortillas. Manuel's wife did not like to do this to the little niña. But the Señor's word was law to her. Felicia patted the rough dough. She put the flat cake on the stove to fry. But she burned her finger.

Felicia would not cry. All those brown children were watching her. She dared not speak for fear she would sob out loud.

But she refused to make more tortillas.

That first day was terrible for poor Felicia.

Then the next day something happened.

Felicia heard Manuel's wife greeting

A MEXICAN GIRL MAKING TORTILLAS

some one at the door. The woman seemed very happy.

"Ah, Dodo, it is you!" cried Manuel's wife. "I knew you would come back. I knew."

Dodo had come back. Dodo had decided to come home, though he knew he should have to serve the Señor's little girls.

But he thought perhaps it might not be so bad as selling water for the potter.

Besides, he liked the little dark girl.

It was only the little light-haired one whom he feared. It was strange to think of Dodo coming home to Manuel's hut with Felicia in Manuel's hut to greet him!

When Dodo first saw Felicia he thought he must be mistaken. She did not wear a pretty frock. Her golden hair was not neatly curled. Her simple apron was soiled.

And she was living in Manuel's poor hut!

Could this be true? Could this be the girl who talked of having Dodo as a mozo? What was she doing here?

Later, Manuel's wife explained to Dodo what had happened.

"She is being punished, the poor niña," said Manuel's wife to Dodo. "She must stay with us until she learns to behave."

"What did she do?" asked Dodo curiously.

"Ah, the Señor says she is not good. She will not obey the Señor. She does not like to work," replied the woman.

"I did not know that Señoritas must work," said Dodo.

Manuel's wife shook her head and shrugged her shoulders. She did not understand it either.

Dodo was sent to serve Dolores.

He went to the big house and he was dressed in clean white trousers and a new cotton shirt. He looked very nice indeed.

But Dolores said, "I do not wish you to serve me. But come into the patio and talk to me."

Dodo followed her into the shady court.

HE STOOD LAZILY AGAINST THE DOORS

"Now, tell me about my sister," Dolores said. "Is she happy?"

Dodo did not know. He could only say that the little blond niña was very quiet.

"That does not sound like Felicia," sighed Dolores. "She must be very sad."

"But," continued Dodo, "she is stubborn. She will not work. And she is very cross."

Dolores smiled.

"Ah, that is more like my sister," she thought to herself.

She gave Dodo a letter to take to Felicia. She wrote comforting words. When he came back to the hut, Dodo found Felicia crying. He handed her the letter. She snatched it from him and read it through.

Then she said, "My sister may not want you to serve her. But when I go home you shall be *my* mozo."

Dodo did not answer. Somehow, he did not fear the girl so much any more.

Dodo had nothing to do all day now, and

"YOU NEVER WORKED IN YOUR LIFE"

he was very happy. He slept contentedly most of the time. Or he lay on his back under the trees and dreamed. Or he stood lazily against doors.

Occasionally he did long to have some clay and paints. But it did not matter so very much.

Felicia watched the lazy boy and he made her very angry.

"Why don't you help with the work, you lazy thing? When you are my mozo I shall make you work!" declared Felicia.

"I shall not be your mozo," said Dodo. "You will never have a mozo because you will never go back to the Señor's house."

Felicia's eyes flashed.

"I will!" she cried. "How do you know?"

Dodo answered, "I know that your father said you must learn to work before you may go back. That you will never learn."

Felicia was very, very angry.

To have this common boy talking to her thus made her cheeks flame with rage. After all, how dare he even talk to her at all!

"You are a fine one to talk of work!" scoffed Felicia. "You never worked in your whole life!"

But Dodo was once more asleep.

BUT DODO WAS ASLEEP

A few days later Felicia came upon Dodo leaning against the hut. He was looking at something which he held in his hands. It was a little clay figure.

"What is that?" asked Felicia.

Dodo handed her the image he had made of Dolores. It was the same image he had made that day at the potter's.

"Why, this is my sister's face!" exclaimed Felicia.

"Si," answered Dodo.

"But—but where did you get it?" the girl inquired.

"I made it," replied Dodo.

"You?" Felicia cried. "I don't believe you!"

"It is true," was all that Dodo said.

He said it so that Felicia had to believe him. She examined the little figure. It was really a beautiful thing. Dodo had even painted it, and the coloring was dainty and charming.

"This is very pretty," Felicia said.

Dodo did not know enough to thank her for these words of praise. But they made him feel very proud nevertheless.

"I should like to show this to my father," continued Felicia.

"I made it for the Señorita Dolores," Dodo announced.

"I MADE IT"

"Why don't you give it to her?" asked Felicia.

"Because I do not know if she will like it," he said.

Felicia could not help smiling.

"Of course she will like it," answered the

girl. "It is very lovely. I should like one, too."

"I do not model now," Dodo told her. "I went away from the potter's where I made this image. I did not like to stay. But I used to make many nice things when I was there."

"Why did you leave?" asked Felicia.

"Because," said Dodo, "they made me work. I do not like to work. It is not fun."

Felicia thought to herself, "Those were the very words I said to my father."

Aloud she asked Dodo, "But don't you like to model and paint?"

Dodo replied, "Yes, of course I do. But that is not work."

"Oh," was all Felicia could say.

She was thinking of her guitar. She was thinking how she had refused to play for Dolores to sing. Really, it was no more work than modeling. Besides, she loved her music. Only she did not like to practice.

"Why don't you model and paint if you like it so much?" she asked Dodo.

"Because," he answered, "they will not teach me unless I work hard. If I agree to peddle water all day, then the potter will teach me. But if I do not work and bring him money, he will not teach me. So I came home to Manuel."

"And you gave up your modeling?" asked Felicia.

"Si, I gave it up," the boy said. "But it makes me sad."

"Then why don't you work for it?" Felicia inquired.

She thought of her father's words: "Perhaps you will learn that everything we do need not be fun."

"Why don't you work if you want to be a potter?" Felicia repeated.

Dodo was silent for a moment.

Then he asked, "Why don't you work if you wish to go back to your home?"

CHAPTER XV

FELICIA REPENTS

Felicia was still angry with Dodo. He was the laziest boy she had ever met.

She thought of the beautiful work he could be doing if he were not so lazy. That made her still angrier. But his words had made her think of herself as well.

It was true that her father would allow her to go home if she would learn to work.

So the next day she said to Manuel's wife, "Please teach me to cook, and to sweep, and to wash. I wish to learn."

Felicia did learn.

She kept thinking to herself, "I would not be so lazy as that Dodo for anything! It is terrible to be so lazy!"

She was pleased with herself when she

could make tortillas as well as Manuel's wife. Manuel told Señor Gallego all about it.

"The little niña is so changed," smiled Manuel, showing all his teeth. "She works so hard and helps in the house. She even cares for the baby. And she washes clothes at the stream. She is a very fine niña!"

Señor Gallego decided that Felicia's punishment was nearly over.

But that afternoon Dodo brought a letter to the Señor. It was from Felicia. It read: "Dear Daddy:

I think I can come home now. I have learned to work. And I think I have learned that practicing music is really not work. I want to practice my music a whole lot. So please, daddy, let me come home.

Your loving daughter,
Felicia.

P.S. I'll never fight any more.

P.S. again. And I won't ever be proud either."

Señor Gallego had a good laugh. Then he called his wife, and they both had a good laugh together.

"I'll go over now and fetch her," said the Señor.

He asked Dolores if she wanted to go along. Dolores was overjoyed.

"Oh, daddy, it will be so wonderful to have Felicia back!" she cried. "It has been so quiet here without her."

"Well, it won't be quiet any more, chick," said Señor Gallego. "Your sister is going to fill the house with music."

When they reached Manuel's hut, Felicia ran out to meet them.

"Daddy, daddy," she exclaimed happily. She threw her arms about her father's neck.

"Do you forgive me, chickadee?" asked the Señor, pulling her hair gently.

"I don't have to forgive you, daddy," Felicia replied. "I'm glad you did it to me. I know now what it means to have a good bed to sleep in—and nice things to eat. I learned about real work."

"Yes?" smiled Señor Gallego. "And what did you learn?"

"Why, practicing isn't real work at all," Felicia told him. "Now I know what real work is. It isn't hard to do the things you love to do. Even Dodo agrees with that."

"Who is Dodo?" asked her father.

"He is the laziest boy that ever lived," replied Felicia, suddenly her old angry self once more. "And I want him to come home with us now and serve me!"

"Ah, Felicia," said her father, "I thought you had learned not to act that way."

"Well, I want to make him work," Felicia explained. "Oh, he can do such beautiful things, daddy, but he won't try at all!"

Señor Gallego saw that Felicia was at last thinking of someone besides herself. The twinkle appeared again in his eye.

"I see," he answered. "Your friend is now

THEY FOUND DODO FAST ASLEEP

a Mexi*can't* and you wish to make him a Mexi*can!* Is that it?"

The girls laughed.

"Yes, that's it, daddy," said Felicia. "And I have a plan, too. But first I want you to meet Dodo. Come with me."

She led her father and sister to the back of the house. There they found Dodo fast asleep. His head was pillowed on a rock.

"Dodo!" called Felicia. "Wake up. My father and Señorita Dolores are here."

The lazy boy opened first one eye and then the other. When he saw the Señor and the little Señoritas standing above him, he jumped up blinking.

"Come, come," laughed Señor Gallego, "do not be alarmed."

"I was asleep," Dodo explained.

"Oh, not really!" the Señor teased. "Why I can hardly believe that. We thought you were fishing."

Then he continued, "But it is always that way when one lies on a rock."

"What do you mean, daddy?" asked Dolores.

"The rock always rocks you to sleep, of course," laughed the Señor. "That's what happened to Dodo."

"DO NOT BE ALARMED"

Dodo could not understand this as it was said in English. The boy just stood rubbing his eyes. Then Felicia turned to him.

"Will you get the little clay image of my sister and bring it here?" she asked.

When Dodo brought the figure of Dolores, the Señor was amazed.

"But did you really do this yourself?" he questioned Dodo.

"Yes, he really did, daddy," Felicia broke in. "And he can do lots of other beautiful things, too. But he is too lazy to work."

"So what do you suggest doing to him?" her father asked.

"I want him to work for me," Felicia repeated.

"But how will that help him to model and paint?" inquired the Señor.

"Oh, he will not have to be a mozo for me," Felicia explained. "I want him to be my private potter. And I want him to model beautiful figures and jars and things."

"Yes, and what else does my spoiled princess want?" interrupted her father. "I thought you had learned a lesson, Felicia."

"You don't understand, daddy," she said. "I did learn a lesson. And I learned it from Dodo. It is terrible to see people so lazy when they can make things like this."

"DID YOU REALLY DO THIS YOURSELF?"

She touched the pretty little clay figure. Then she went on, "So I want him to make lots more. They won't be for me at all, but for himself. He shall go to market with his donkey and sell his wares. I want him to be a great potter some day. But he won't be unless he learns to work."

CHAPTER XVI
POTTER DODO

It was like Fairyland at the hacienda.

The patio was a mass of flowers and laughing children.

Gay-colored birds flew all about. Music sounded.

It was the birthday of Felicia and Dolores.

The twins sat in a corner of the patio. They wore their Spanish costumes. Felicia strummed upon her guitar. Dolores began to sing. The guests gathered around and listened.

The two girls were lovely to look at.

Dolores smiled as she sang.

Some one whispered, "Isn't she like an old Mexican picture?"

Felicia played her guitar as though she loved it.

Felicia had been practicing everyday since her return from Manuel's house. Now she could play so well that people were surprised.

It was all Dodo's doing. Lazy little Dodo had so angered Felicia that she had determined never to be like him. So she had worked.

She had done something else besides. She had done something for Dodo because she wanted to help him.

"Come, everyone," called Felicia when they had finished their song. "I want to show you my little potter."

Felicia and Dolores led their guests to the garden. There stood a tiny house. It was hardly larger than a doll's house. It was under a big tree. It was Dodo's workshop.

But Dodo also had a little tree house where he loved to sit and work. It was only a bench set in the trees but it was his favorite place.

THE GIRLS WERE LOVELY TO LOOK AT

He was happy. Dodo was happy at last, and all because of Felicia. Little proud Felicia had helped little sleepy Dodo.

Besides, Dodo had learned something from Felicia. He had discovered that the rich girl could play the guitar very nicely. He had seen her begin to practice without complaining. He had begun to like Felicia. He had begun to admire her.

Then she had talked very crossly to Dodo.

"My father will build you a place where you may model and paint," Felicia had said to him. "But you must work and not sleep all day. You must sell your wares at market as other potters do."

Señor Gallego had had a potter come each day to teach Dodo about modeling. But soon the potter had said, "He knows as much as I do now. He is already a master."

Dodo was busy all day long.

By the side of the tiny house stood Amigo. Almost every day Dodo went to market with

DODO HAD A LITTLE TREE BENCH

his pottery piled on Amigo's back. Dodo did not have to carry a load of pottery on his back as some boys do in Mexico. He had the donkey to help him.

Amigo seemed as happy as Dodo himself when they sold much pottery. The little donkey was a faithful friend to Dodo and would never forget that the boy had saved him from an unhappy life. They say that donkeys are stupid and stubborn. If so, they are also faithful and friendly.

Dodo sold vases and dishes and jars. He felt very proud and did not want to sleep his days away any more.

Felicia and Dolores now led their party guests to Dodo's pottery house. All the children were interested in the young potter of whom they had heard.

They found Dodo painting in his tree.

"Dodo, may we see your works?" Felicia inquired.

"Si, si," replied the boy. His white teeth glistened as he smiled. His dark eyes lit with pleasure.

He showed the children his pretty pottery. They exclaimed with joy.

"IT IS FOR YOU, SEÑORITA"

Felicia said, "If you will each select something, I will buy it for you."

Señor Gallego had given Felicia some money on her birthday. She was using it this way. It was a fine way to use it. Everyone was pleased. Dodo was pleased. Each little guest picked out a dainty bit of pottery and was delighted with it. But Señor Gallego was the happiest of all to see how unselfish Felicia had become. Suddenly Dodo held out a package to Felicia.

"It is for you, Señorita," he said. "For your birthday."

Then he gave another package to Dolores.

"And for you, too, Señorita," he added.

All the little guests were anxious to see what Dodo had given to the twins.

Dolores opened her package first. She gave a cry of delight. Dodo had modeled a perfect image of the little dog, Five Toes.

"Oh, it has just his saucy little face!" Dolores exclaimed.

All the children had to examine it. They agreed that it was just like the funny hairless dog. Then Felicia opened her package.

The guests crowded around, anxious to see what Dodo had given the other sister.

Imagine their surprise and delight when Felicia held up a clay figure of herself play-

"YOU ARE VERY PRETTY WHEN YOU PLAY THE GUITAR"

ing the guitar. It was so perfect that the children all said, "Oh!" at once.

Felicia said to Dodo, "This is the loveliest gift I ever received. But I don't deserve it. I have been very cross to you."

But Dodo smiled from ear to ear. It seemed his smile would never rub off.

"It was you who helped me, Señorita," he answered.

This made Felicia very happy. She thought, of course, that Dodo meant the tiny house, and the clay, and the tools that she had given him.

But she was surprised when Dodo said, "I learned a great lesson from you, Señorita. I learned to work hard, and not be lazy as you were!"

Felicia could hardly believe her ears.

So this boy had been as disgusted with her as she had been with him!

Dodo went on, "I saw you play the guitar, and I thought, 'What a pity! She plays so very nicely, and she will not practice.'

"Then you practiced. And I said, 'If this lazy girl can practice, then I can work.'

"Then you gave me tools and clay. Now I do not sleep any more, but I work instead.

"You are very pretty when you play the guitar. So I made this little gift for you."

CHAPTER XVII

ADIOS

Dodo became a great potter. Felicia became a good lady. Many people from far and near visited the hacienda. They came to see Dodo's works and to have their images made in clay.

Dodo stayed on the hacienda because he liked it there and because Felicia wanted him to stay. The Gallego family decided to remain in Mexico. They did not go back to the United States at all.

Señor Gallego was just as interested in Dodo as were his daughters. He treated him like a son. He made him go to school and learn. Also he tried to find out who the boy's parents had been.

At last he did find out. Dodo's father had

been an Indian potter and his mother had been a Spanish lady.

Dodo was a real Mexican boy, a mestizo, the kind that are helping to build Mexico today.

But they never learned Dodo's last name. Dodo did not like the name Sleepyhead because he was not sleepy any more.

So Señor Gallego said one day, "Let us find a good name for Dodo—a name that suits him."

The Señor thought awhile. Then he said, "I know a good name for Dodo. We shall call him Juan (hwän) because it means 'light at last.' "

The girls did not quite understand, so the Señor explained.

"You see," he said, "Dodo has been sleeping most of his life away. Now he has opened his eyes and sees the light at last."

When he was old enough Dodo married Felicia. They bought all the hard-worked

"ADIOS"

donkeys that they could find and gave them a good home on the hacienda.

Dodo wanted to do this because, as he said, "One of my best friends was a little donkey."

Dolores adopted a baby from the Cuna, the orphan asylum that Dodo came from. And she helped many other babies to find good homes.

So we shall leave them now.

And if they were to bid you good-bye they would use the pretty Mexican farewell—
"ADIOS"

PRONOUNCING VOCABULARY

Adios . . . . ä′dyōs′

Amigo . . . . ä-mē′gō

Chapultepec . . . . chä-pōōl′tä-pĕk′

Charro . . . . chär′rō

Chihuahua . . . . chế-wä′wä

Chirimoya . . . . chĭr′ĭ-moi′à

Cuna . . . . kōō′nà

Dolores . . . . dō-lōr′ēz

Dodo . . . . dō′dō

El Toro . . . . ĕl tō′rō

Felicia . . . . fē-lĭsh′ĭ-à

Fiesta . . . . fyĕs′tä

Gallego . . . . gäl-yä′gō

Garcia . . . . gär-thē′à

Guadalajara . . . . gwä′thä-lä-hä′rä

Guanajuato . . . . gwä′nä-hwä′tō

Hacienda . . . . hä-sĭ-ĕn′dä

Ixtaccihuatl . . . . ēs-täk-sē′hwät'l

Juan . . . . hwän

Manuel . . . . măn′ū-ĕl

Maximilian . . . . măk′sĭ-mĭl′yăn

223

Maguey . . . . măg'wā
Maya . . . . mä'yä
Mestizo . . . . měs-tē'zō
Monterrey . . . . mŏn'ter-rā'
Mozo . . . . mō'zō
Nieve . . . . nē-ā'vā
Niño . . . . nēn'yō
Paseo de la Reforma . . pä-sā'ō de lä rā-fôr'mä
Patio . . . . pät'yō
Pedro . . . . pā'drō
Popocatepetl . . . . pō-pō'kä-tā'pět'l
Pulque . . . . pōol'kä
Queretaro . . . . kā-rā'tä-rō
San Luis Potosi . . . . sän lŏo-ēs'pō-tō-sē'
Señor . . . . sā-nyōr'
Señora . . . . sā-nyō'rä
Señoritas . . . . sā'nyō-rē'täs
Serape . . . . sĕ-rä'pä
Si . . . . sē
Sierra Madre . . . . sĭ-ĕr'à mä'drä
Sombrero . . . . sŏm-brā'rō
Tamale . . . . tà-mä'lĕ
Texcoco . . . . täs-kō'kō
Tortillas . . . . tōr-tēl'yäs